MW01138742

Double Trouble

From the Tales of Dan Coast

By: Rodney Riesel

Published by Island Holiday Publishing
East Greenbush, NY

ISBN: 978-0-9894877-9-5
First Edition

Special thanks to:
Pamela Guerriere
Kevin Cook

Cover Design by:
Connie Fitsik

To learn about my other books friend me at
https://www.facebook.com/rodneyriesel

For Brenda,
Kayleigh, Ethan
& Peyton

KEY LARGO

ISLAMORADA

MARATHON

BIG PINE KEY &
THE LOWER KEYS

KEY WEST

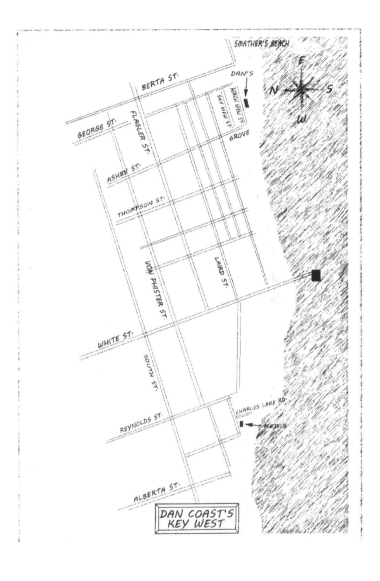

SMATHER'S BEACH

BERTA ST.

DAN'S

SKY VIEW ST.

GROVE

GEORGE ST.

FLAGLER ST.

ASHBY ST.

THOMPSON ST.

VON PHISTER ST.

LAIRD ST.

WHITE ST.

SOUTH ST.

CHARLES LAKE RD.

REYNOLDS ST.

RED'S

ALBERTA ST.

DAN COAST'S
KEY WEST

Chapter One

Dan Coast and Red Baxter drove along US1 in Key Largo. Red was behind the wheel of his gold 1975 Firebird. "Ya know, I kinda *feel* like Jim Rockford when I'm driving this baby," Red said.

Dan glanced over. Rolling his eyes he said, "Yeah, I can see that. I don't remember Rockford having that gut, and I don't think they ever mentioned his hairy back on the show."

"For your information, I had my back shaved yesterday."

"Good to know," Dan said, pointing his finger. "Turn right up here."

Red veered left onto Ocean Bay Drive. "Hey, a Burger King!" he announced.

"Maybe when we're done here … *if* you're a good boy."

"How far up?"

"Take the next left."

Red turned, drove up a block, and then took another left onto Point Pleasant Drive.

About halfway down the street Dan said, "Pull over right here and we'll walk the rest of the way."

Red veered off the road into the grass and shut off the engine. "Who lives here?" he asked.

"No one," Dan answered. "That's what made me think it might be a good place to park." He turned and grabbed the black leather bag from the back seat and placed it on his lap. Unzipping the bag he removed a camera.

"Wow. Where did you get that?" Red asked.

"Amazon."

"The jungle, or the web site?"

"Funny." Dan pulled out a six-inch attachment and fastened it to the front of the camera.

"What's that?"

"Night vision adapter," Dan answered, with a child-like, Christmas morning grin. "And this here is a telephoto lens." He attached the lens to the night vision adapter, making the entire camera about seventeen-inches long.

"Looks like a cannon," Red pointed out.

"Nope, it's a Nikon," said Dan.

"How much did that set you back?"

"A little over six grand."

"Jesus!"

"It came with this free leather bag," Dan said defensively.

"Not too long ago you thought a hundred bucks for a smart phone was too much. Now you lay down six grand for a camera and a few lenses. How much are you even making on this job?"

"Five hundred bucks." Dan opened the door and got out. "Come on."

"Not very cost effective." Red climbed out and together they walked down the side of the street.

Dan Coast didn't have to worry about cost effectiveness. Since he had won the lottery years ago, he could afford a freewheeling lifestyle that included all the debauchery and gadgets his little heart desired. The windfall also allowed him to indulge in his favorite hobby: playing amateur detective, his role models being the TV sleuths he couldn't get enough of.

When they got to the last house on the right Dan said, "Here's the place."

The front of the house, and driveway, faced Bayview Drive. The left side of the house overlooked the Gulf. Surrounding the property was a six-foot-high block wall that had been stuccoed and recently painted white. The house was white and stuccoed as well. Dan and Red peeked over the block wall from the Point Pleasant Drive side of the property into the side yard. An in-ground pool took up most of the yard.

In the darkness, two figures moved about the pool. They spoke quietly and giggled several times.

"I'm guessing those two playing grab ass in the pool are *not* husband and wife, or we wouldn't be here," Red surmised.

"Good guess," Dan responded. "The husband, Charles Hamilton, is in Miami this evening, on business." Dan raised the lens up over the top of the fence and snapped a few pictures without looking through the view finder. "Charles is fifty-two years old, so is his wife Tiffany. That's Tiffany in the pool. I'm not sure of the name of the thirty-something-year-old flotation device that she's riding."

"Hey, you're pretty good with that thing," Red observed. "Who showed you how to use it?"

"No one. The description on Amazon said that it was so easy, even a child could do it." Dan crouched back down and looked at the display screen.

"They probably meant a normal child, not a grown man with the *mind* of a child."

Dan began hitting buttons. "How the hell do you look at the pictures?"

"I guess we should have brought a child."

"How about if you wait in the car?"

"Give me that thing!" said Red, yanking the camera from his technologically challenged friend's hands. He tapped a button and turned the camera back toward Dan and whispered, "Push this button with the arrow to look through the pics."

"Thanks." Dan scanned through the five photographs he had just taken. There was one of the barbecue grill, two of the back door, one of the deck railing, and one of a figure swimming around in the pool.

Red peered over Dan's shoulder at the pictures. "Great job," he said sarcastically.

"Got one of someone in the pool."

"That looks just like every murky photo I've ever seen of the Loch Ness Monster. Maybe you should try aiming the camera at what you're photographing, laddie"

"Yeah, maybe," Dan agreed.

"And turn on the night vision thing this time."

Dan stood, pointed the camera at the two swimmers, and started taking pictures. When he was finished he dropped back down next to Red. "Cool," he whispered.

"What's cool?"

"The pictures are green, just like that Paris Hilton sex tape ... and just as naked." Dan stood again and took a few more.

Red jumped up and looked over the fence. "Give me the camera, I can't see anything."

"You don't need to see anything, ya pervert."

"I'm a pervert, but you're not?"

"I'm getting paid by a jealous husband to catch his wife getting dicked on the sly. That's the difference between a pervert and a professional," Dan stated, snapping away.

"If I'd known you were gonna hog all the fun on this caper I wouldn't have tagged along."

"Okay, okay, here," he said, handing Red the Nikon. "Let's go around by the gate."

The two men duck-walked around the corner onto Bayview Drive. When they entered the driveway the white marble stone crunched beneath their feet.

"Shh," Dan said, his finger to his lips.

"Sorry," Red whispered. He glanced over at the black Ford Mustang in the driveway. "Should we get a few shots of the car?"

"Good idea."

Red turned and snapped a few of the car and then a couple of the rear license plate. He returned his attention to the gate.

Dan lifted the latch and carefully pulled open the gate. With the side of his foot he raked some stone in front of the gate to hold it open.

They entered the yard on a red brick pathway lined with buttonwood shrubs. Red stuck the lens through the silvery foliage and began taking pictures. After he had snapped off fifty or sixty shots he handed the camera back to Dan. "Wow," he said. "Why can't I find a woman like that?"

Dan gave Red a sideways look. "Your ex-wife was *just* like that."

"Yeah, with *other* guys. I need a woman who will let *me* do things like that to her."

Dan put the camera back to his eye and gave a low whistle of admiration. "That might be illegal," he commented, as he watched the couple thrashing about amorously in the water.

Red grabbed the camera. "Let me see."

Dan yanked it back. "Let go."

"Is someone there?" they heard a woman call out.

Dan looked through the view finder and saw the young bare-assed man pulling himself out of the pool. He went to the pool house, flipped a switch, and the entire property lit up like a prison yard during a jail break.

"Time to go!" Dan said.

"Who's there," the young man hollered.

"Sex police!" Red shouted. "Nobody move! Hands above your head!"

The naked fellow froze and threw his arms skyward as Dan and Red disappeared into the darkness.

As the two men ran back down Point Pleasant Drive

toward the car Dan turned to Red. "How come you never mentioned you were with the sex police?" he asked jokingly.

"Didn't want to blow my cover."

Chapter Two

Red balanced a large order of onion rings on his left knee and his half-eaten Double Whopper with cheese on his right as he noisily sucked his soda through his straw.

Dan watched in disgusted amazement as they cruised along US1. "I swear, you've gained five pounds in the last ten minutes," he said.

"I swear ... you ... should shut up," Red replied with one of his usual lackluster comebacks.

"Good one."

Red took another bite of his burger and a glob of ketchup splattered on his blue Hawaiian shirt. "I can't believe you didn't want anything."

"I can't believe it either. I hear people come to the Keys from all over the world just to experience the Burger King's."

Red took another bite and a second splatter of ketchup hit the shirt. "Dammit! We should have eaten there."

Dan glanced over at the crimson splotch on his buddy's shirt. "You should have worn your red Hawaiian shirt." He grabbed the wheel as Red unsuccessfully attempted to clean up his mess.

"I got it," Red groused as he took the wheel back.

Dan let go and slumped back in his seat. "I could have driven."

"You don't have a license."

"I didn't forget how to drive."

"Is Maxine meeting you at my place?" Red asked, referring to Dan's comely lady friend, a nurse who'd become tangled in Dan's exploits—the same ones that cost him his driving privileges—a few months back.

"Yup. I told her we should be back around ten."

Red looked at his watch. "Should be."

"Just watch the road." Dan reached over and tuned the radio to 104.1. Van Morrison was belting out "Into the Mystic." "Love this song."

As Dan sang along with Van he noticed that Red kept checking the rear view mirror more frequently than usual. He glanced into the passenger side mirror but couldn't see anything.

Red shoved the last of his Whopper into his pork trap, wadded up the wrapper, and tossed it over his shoulder into the back seat. He checked the mirror once more.

"Something wrong?" Dan asked.

"Not sure," Red answered, and shoved the three remaining onion rings into his mouth.

Dan turned around and looked out the back window. "What are they doing?"

"Came up kind of fast and then stayed back for a

while. In the last few minutes they drove up close and then backed off a couple times."

"Maybe they're pissed because you're not going fast enough."

Red glanced at his speedometer. "I'm doing sixty."

"Slow down a little and see what they do."

Red slowed and as the distance between the vehicles lessened Red rolled down his window, stuck out his arm, and motioned for them to pass. The car slowed as well. Red sped up. "They're fuckin' with me."

"Floor it and put some distance between us."

Red did, and the car behind them accelerated and rode the Firebird's bumper. "Hang on!" He slammed on the brakes.

The car swerved into the left lane and Red jumped on the gas again. The vehicle came up beside them. It was the same black Mustang that was parked in the Hamiltons' driveway. Red gave Dan a surprised look and then pushed the pedal all the way to the floor.

Seconds later the Mustang regained its position beside them. Red glanced over and the window of the Ford lowered. An arm reached through the window and the chrome barrel of a .45 gleamed as the vehicles passed under a street light.

Red fumbled with the window crank and the barrel flashed, sending lead through the car, shattering the passenger side window.

"What the Christ!" Dan screamed.

Red hit the brakes and threw the Firebird into reverse. Dan watched as the Mustang hit its brakes and swerved across both lanes. Red pressed on the gas, and when he had reached thirty miles an hour, hit the brakes again and spun the wheel hard right, pulled the shifter into drive, and floored it. The ass end of the car swung around and they were headed north again.

"Holy shit! You are Rockford!" Dan shouted.

Red took a right into a Dairy Queen parking lot, across US1 North, and onto Garden Street. "Good thing Cindy shaved my back!" he shouted, jokingly.

Dan cringed. "You made that poor girl shave your back?"

Red took a left and then another left onto Arbor Lane. "Yeah, for fifty bucks."

"Not a bargain."

They flew through the Circle K parking lot and back onto the highway heading south. As they drove past the Dairy Queen again, Red saw the Mustang drive by in the north bound lane.

Red stabbed a stubby finger at the car. "There they are!"

"Did they see us?' Dan asked.

They watched as their pursuers turned onto Arbor Lane.

"I don't think so." Red pressed the gas pedal to the floor. "But you better add in a new passenger side window when you bill this guy."

As they crossed the bridge and passed the Tavernier Creek Marina the lights of a cop car flashed and lit up the rear-view mirror. Red slammed his hands down on the steering wheel.

"You can also add in the price of this ticket."

Chapter Three

When he awoke, Dan Coast was lying on his back in his hammock. He was wearing a blue concert T, The Tubes, a ratty relic from the eighties. Love Bomb, the name of the group's album, was printed across the front. A small red blanket was draped across him. His right leg hung off the edge of the hammock and his arms were outstretched above his head.

He opened his eyes slowly, thanking God that it was cloudy. His mouth felt like he had eaten a cotton ball sandwich. With a groan he rolled over and reached for the almost empty Dos Manos tequila bottle that lay on the ground beneath him, between a purple bra with cream colored lace, a size six woman's sneaker, and a few other articles of clothing that had been hurriedly removed during a drunken sex frenzy.

Dan put the bottle to his lips, drank the last three shots, and tossed the bottle toward the fire pit, it missed and hit the ground with a thud. He stretched his arms toward the sky and shivered. It was sixty-five degrees out, Dan remembered back to when he lived in New York and considered sixty-five a warm spring day. Now living in Florida for a few years, his blood having thinned, as they say, he thought about putting on a sweater.

His screen door slammed. "Finally awake?" Maxine asked.

Dan grumbled some unintelligible response.

"What was that?" she asked.

He grabbed the edge of the hammock and pulled himself up. *Holy shit!* The world wasn't quite done spinning and his brain hadn't yet reattached itself to the inside of his skull.

Smirking, Maxine said, "One too many. Told you so."

Dan rubbed the tiny, puffy slits he called eyes and then ran his fingers through his short hair. "You're chipper this morning."

"That's because I know when to quit drinking."

"I wish you would have told me when to quit."

"I tried. You called me an amateur and a quitter. You're a real asshole when you're that drunk."

"I never said I wasn't." Dan stood and wobbled a bit, his stomach wanted to make a quick exit through his dry mouth.

"Maybe you should have just come home last night after the big car chase instead of getting shit-faced."

"Yeah, I'll keep that in mind for the next time," Dan said. He rubbed his temples with his finger and thumb. "Wanna walk down to the beach and take a quick dip?"

"No, you go ahead. I just started breakfast. It'll be ready by the time you get back up here."

"Eggs?" Dan asked.

"Yes."

"Can you make them scrambled? I don't think I can stomach yolks today."

"I thought you would love some yellow, runny, yolks and maybe I could under-cook them a bit so there would be some of that white snotty stuff running around the plate,"

Dan held up one hand and put the other over his mouth. "Please." He started to walk toward the beach.

"Are you going to put some pants on?"

Dan looked down at what dangled. "Maybe I better." He pulled on his tan cargo shorts and staggered to the beach.

Buddy, Dan's black Lab/Border collie mix, jumped up from the deck of his next-door neighbor, Bev, picked up the tennis ball at the bottom of the steps and ran as fast as he could to join his "master" on the beach.

Dan was up to his ankles in the water when Buddy entered at full speed, splashing Dan with the cool morning water.

"Jesus Christ!" Dan yelled. "Quit splashing around."

Buddy paid no attention to Dan's request and dropped the tennis ball in the water next to him.

"Oh, I'll throw the ball all right," Dan said, picking it up. "See if I can't throw it out near a shark." He let the ball fly into the ocean. Buddy gave chase.

Dan waded out until he was up to his waist and then dove in. He swam under water as long as he could hold his breath and then slowly surfaced. He wiped the water from his face and turned back toward shore.

By this time Buddy was on the beach, digging in the sand, his tennis ball a few feet away.

What the hell is that dog digging up now? Dan thought and dove back in. He swam to the bottom and pushed himself back toward the surface. When he stood the water was chest deep. He walked back toward shore and called out to his dog: "Get the ball, dog."

Buddy paid no attention and kept digging.

Dan reached the shore. *What the hell is that?* "Buddy get over here!"

Buddy stopped digging and ran to Dan.

"What you got over here, pal?" Dan walked to where Buddy was digging. Sticking out of the sand was an arm. "Shit!"

Dan dropped to his knees and raked back some sand with his fingers. The body of a man, dead long enough to be stiff, but not long enough to stink, lay on his back. Someone had tried to bury him in a hurry and didn't do a very good job. Dan guessed the man to be in his late thirties. His hair was dark and cut short; his complexion, whatever hue it might have been when he was alive, was now blue. The man was wearing jeans but no shirt or shoes. Dan dug underneath the man and reached into his back pocket. No wallet.

"Dan!" he heard Maxine call out from the back yard.

Dan looked up from the corpse and Maxine was walking his way. Dan jumped to his feet and walked quickly to Maxine. "You don't want to go down there," he said.

Maxine tried to look over Dan's shoulder. "Why, what's the matter?" She tried to side-step him but Dan grabbed her arm.

"It's a body," he said, "Don't look. It ain't pretty."

"A body?"

21

"A dead body."

"Who is it?"

"He doesn't have any ID on him."

"Are you sure he's dead?"

Dan raised one eye brow. "Oh he's dead alright. Been dead a few hours at least." He headed toward the house. "Come on."

"Where are you going?"

"Call the cops and eat my breakfast."

"Should we just leave him there?"

"He ain't going nowhere."

When Dan got to his back door he held it open for Buddy and Maxine. He knew leaving Buddy outside with a dead body, unattended, was probably a bad idea. Dan and Maxine walked through the kitchen and into the dining room. Buddy kept walking straight into the living room and lay down on his puffy flannel bed next to the small table with an elegantly framed photograph of Dan's late wife.

Maxine pointed at the dining room table. "Your breakfast is ready when you are."

Dan glanced over at the two plates filled with scrambled eggs, sausage, and toast. There was a part of him that wanted to eat first and phone the police after. He sighed. "Where's my cell phone?" he asked.

"Where did you leave it?" Maxine asked.

"If I knew where I le—" Dan shook his head. "Never mind." The back and forth banter with a woman he cared about was something Dan hadn't experienced in quite a while. He liked it, but it also brought back a lot of emotion he wasn't able to deal with. Dan and Maxine had been together for six months now and the better he got to know her, the more she reminded him of Alex.

He found his phone on the end table next to his La-Z-Boy. *Oh yeah,* he remembered and grabbed it. He searched through his contacts for Rick Carver, Key West's Chief of Police. He hadn't spoken to Rick in about four months and wondered if maybe he should just dial 911.

He dialed Rick's number and while it rang he walked over to his plate and grabbed a piece of sausage, shoving it into his mouth.

"That's my plate," Maxine informed him.

"Then why is it sitting in front of my chair?" Dan asked.

Rick's voice mail picked up and Dan left a message. "Rick, its Dan. How's it going?"

"How's it going?" Maxine echoed. "You might want to start with the dead body thing."

"Hey, ah ... me and my dog went for a swim this morning and we found a dead body on the beach. Call me back." Dan hung up the phone, sat down at the table and began eating breakfast.

Maxine stared at him in disbelief. "That's it?"

"What's it?" Dan asked with a mouthful of eggs.

"I found a dead body, call me back?"

Dan shrugged. "Hey, I did my part. Sit down and eat."

"What if someone else finds the body?"

"No one worried about me finding—" Dan made finger quotes "—*the body.*"

"But you're not the one who left it there," Maxine said. "And that's not where you would use finger quotes."

"Are ya sure I didn't leave it there? I was pretty drunk last night. And I'm pretty sure you can use finger quotes anywhere you want."

Chapter Four

Chief Rick Carver stood at the back of Dan's yard, near the beach. His head slowly turned as he scanned Dan's property, pausing for a second when he noticed the bra, sneaker, and empty tequila bottle that lay under the hammock. He disgustedly shook his head and then turned to gaze out over the Atlantic Ocean.

A forensic technician from the Monroe County Medical Examiner's Office was seated at Dan's picnic table, talking on his cell phone. Two police officers were walking around the beach looking at the sand. Two members of Key West's Crime Scene Unit were moving sand around at the bottom of the shallow hole where the body *used* to be. Dan and Maxine were standing next to Rick. Maxine wanted to retrieve her bra but had been told not to touch anything.

"Okay," Rick said. "Let me get this straight. You were sleeping over here_" He pointed at Dan's hammock and then back at the hole "_and somebody was burying a body over there … and you both slept through it."

Dan nodded yes. "That's about the size of it."

Rick continued. "Then you and your mutt found the body. You called my cell and left a message, instead of calling 911, and then ate your breakfast."

Maxine shook her head yes this time. "That's what happened."

"That's the whole story," Dan agreed.

Rick took a deep breath and slowly let it out. He pushed his gold-rimmed aviators further up the bridge of his sweaty nose with his index finger. "Well that's not exactly the whole story, now, is it? Because then there's the part about me and the rest of these guys getting here and not finding a body."

"Yeah, that's the mystery," Dan deadpanned.

"No," Rick said, shaking his finger at Dan. "The mystery is why this shit always seems to happen around you."

"I guess that would be the second mystery," Dan agreed.

Rick turned and walked over to join his officers on the beach. "Six years till retirement," he muttered.

"I thought you said you two were friends," Maxine stated. "Because, from where I stand, it doesn't really seem like he likes you."

Dan stared out at the beach. "You're probably just standing in the wrong spot. Maybe the sun was in your eyes … because he loves me."

"I think a private detective should have a better working relationship with the local police chief."

"I'm not a private detective."

"I'm just saying."

"I got something!" Rick shouted from the beach. Everyone's head turned as he lowered his massive girth down on to one knee and pulled something from the sand. It was a small piece of paper, he waved it in the air above his head. "A five dollar bill!"

Dan shook his head.

"So what's the first step in this investigation?" Maxine asked.

"What investigation?"

Maxine pointed at the hole in the sand. "The case of the missing dead guy," she said, throwing in a few bars of *The Twilight Zone's* "doo-doo, doo-doo theme for spooky effect.

"The first step is not giving a shit." Dan made a check mark in the air with his finger. "Step one … complete."

"You mean to tell me you're not the slightest bit curious who dug a hole and buried a guy twenty feet from where we were sleeping?"

"As *I* remember it, we weren't just sleeping," Dan recalled with a wink.

"Yeah, pretty much, we were" Maxine recollected.

"We also did it."

"Did it?"

"Yeah … did it. The nasty, knockin' boots, the horizontal mambo, take ol' one eye to th—"

"Okay, okay, I get it, Maxine cut in. "And for your information, we started *doing it* and you fell asleep."

"Ohh, really? I *could* say that's never happened to me before, but we would both know I was lying."

Rick walked back over to Dan and Maxine. Meanwhile, the other officers were also ambling back to

27

Dan's backyard. "I think we're all done here," Rick said. "We haven't found anything unusual, except for you."

Maxine laughed and Dan shot her a look.

Rick put his hand on Maxine's shoulder. "Maxine, darlin', did you actually see the body?"

"Um … no, I didn't actually see it for myself."

Rick looked over at Dan. "That's what I figured." He waved his finger in a circle above his head. "Let's wrap it up!"

Dan stood facing the back of his house, his arms folded in front of him, watching as Key West's finest made their way past his fire pit, past the Adirondack chairs, and up the gravel pathway that led to the driveway. "Um … no, I didn't actually see it for myself," Dan aped.

"Sorry! What was I supposed to say?"

"You could have lied."

"Sorry."

"You *could* make it up to me."

"Oh yeah. How?"

"Maybe we could go in the house and finish what we started in the hammock last night. I promise I won't fall asleep this time."

"Okay, but go take a shower first and brush your teeth."

"Really?"

"Yeah. You smell like a goat."

Chapter Five

"Hey! Long time no see," Red sang out as Dan and Maxine walked through the front door of Red's Bar and Grill.

"Yeah, about ten hours," Dan mumbled. He removed his Ray Bans and even the light inside seemed to be a little too bright.

Maxine hopped up on one of the orange bar stools, Dan climbed aboard the one beside her. She reached over and mussed his hair. "Sonny Boy has a little hangover."

"Coffee?" Red asked.

"Sure," Maxine answered.

"Bloody Mary," Dan growled.

Red grabbed a hurricane glass off a shelf behind the bar, then grabbed a coffee cup and filled it for Maxine. "I didn't think someone like you could get a hangover."

Dan's hackles rose for a fight. "Someone like me? You mean someone of Irish-German descent? That's racist,

29

ya bastard."

Red filled the glass with ice, poured a double shot of vodka. "I meant a raging alcoholic, like you."

"Well, that's just mean," Dan informed him.

"He's a bit touchy today," Maxine stated.

"What the Christ? I'm not touchy."

"See what I mean?"

"Yup," Red agreed. "He doesn't know when to quit drinking, that's his problem."

"That's what I said," Maxine agreed.

"I bet you too don't even realize just how handy it is to have a best friend and a girlfriend who are both psychiatrists."

"Wow! Almost four years and that's the first time he's called me his best friend," Red pointed out.

"Almost six months and that's the first time he's called me his girlfriend."

"You know what his problem is?" Red asked.

"Oh my God!" Dan bawled and climbed off of his bar stool. "I gotta piss, that's my problem right now."

Maxine laughed. "No, what's his problem, Red?"

"Fear of intimacy," Red diagnosed.

Dan lumbered across the floor, his flip-flops sticking to the wooden planks with every step. "You know what your problem is?" he shouted over his shoulder. "You never mop the floor."

When Dan returned and reclaimed his bar stool, Maxine and Red were still laughing. "I'm glad I can provide you two with so much humor," he said, and sipped his Bloody Mary.

"Can I get the two of you something to eat?" Red asked.

"No, thanks, we already ate. I have to be to work at three," Maxine answered, checking the clock on the wall behind the bar.

"We just stopped by to get something to go for Mel," Dan explained.

"Officer Mel Gormin was a policeman only in his mind. Dan had met him during his court-ordered stay in a mental institution—his reward for antics that were even too outlandish for a party town like Key West. Dan and Mel had become pals and teamed up on one of Dan's "cases."

"Good old Officer Mel," Red said. "How's he doing?"

"He's doing good," Maxine responded.

"As good as you can be, locked up in a nut house," Dan added.

Red pulled a guest check pad over in front of him and grabbed the pen that lay next to it. "What can I get him?"

"Cheeseburger, fries, and a large water," Dan answered.

Red looked puzzled. "Water? Don't they have any at the booby hatch?"

"Mel thinks the water there is laced with hallucinogens. He's always carrying on about some conspiracy theory. I humor him."

"Okay, you're the boss." Red jotted the order down, turned, and went through the swinging kitchen door. "Jocko, order up!" he shouted.

Dan took another drink of his Bloody Mary and then pulled the piece of celery from the glass. He tossed the stalk on the bar in front of Maxine. "Here ya go, you can have my salad."

Maxine picked it up and took a bite. "God forbid you should eat a vegetable."

"For your information, this glass is filled with tomato juice and the tomato is a vegetable. Also, the vodka is made from potatoes. I'm pretty much drinking a glass of vegetable soup."

"Yeah, pretty much," Maxine said sarcastically. "And for your information, potatoes aren't vegetables."

"I'm pretty sure they are."

"I'm pretty sure they're not. They're tubers."

"I'm pretty sure I don't give a shit."

"Give a shit about what?" Red asked when he returned to the bar.

"Nothing," Dan answered.

"He thinks potatoes are vegetables," Maxine said.

"I'm pretty sure they are," Red stated.

Maxine took another bite of the celery. "They're not. And now that I think about it, the tomato is technically a fruit that's often eaten as a vegetable."

Red shrugged. "Ah, who gives a shit."

"Exactly!" Dan said, and slid his glass back across the bar. "Fill 'er up, sir."

"Another Bloody Mary?" Red asked.

"Yeah," Dan responded. "But put tequila in this one and instead of tomato juice, maybe a little 7Up."

"And let me guess: a lime?"

"You got it, pal."

Red made the drink and slid the glass back. "More coffee, Maxine?" he asked.

"Yes, please," she answered, and then jumped off of her stool and went toward the ladies room.

Red watched with open appreciation of Maxine's ass as she crossed the floor and disappeared through the door, then, he turned back to Dan. "Hey, some guy was in here about an hour before you two got here. He sat at the bar and had a couple drinks. He asked if I knew you."

"No one you've ever seen before?" Dan asked.

"No, he wasn't from around here. I told him I knew you and that you would probably be in tonight around six for dinner."

"What did he want with me?"

"Don't know."

"He say where he got my name?"

"No, and I didn't ask."

"Looks like I'll be back for dinner."

The kitchen door swung open and Jocko walked up to the bar with Dan's order in a to-go bag. "This for you, Coast?"

"Sure is, Jocko. Thanks."

Jocko sat the bag in front of Dan and then took a seat on the stool at the end of the bar. As usual, a nasty-looking cigar, more spit than tobacco, dangled from the cook's pug-ugly puss. Red grabbed an ashtray and put it front of him. "Can you pour me a ginger-ale, boss?" he asked Red.

Red grabbed a glass, filled it with ice, and sat it next to the ash tray.

Jocko pulled the disgusting stogie from his mouth, laid it on the ashtray, and took a big swig of his soda.

"Where's that little filly of yours, Coast?"

"She's in the bathroom."

"I figured you two weren't too far apart."

"What's that supposed to mean?" Dan asked.

"She seems to keep you on a pretty short leash these days. Didn't think you were the type that could be tamed so easily."

"I'm not," Dan argued.

"That's what all the pussy-whipped men say."

Red was grinning from ear to ear. There was nothing that made him happier than watching Dan *get* some of the medicine he was usually *giving.*

Maxine exited the restroom and returned to her seat. When she saw the smiles on Jocko and Red's face she asked, "What did I miss?"

Jocko reached his massive arm over the corner of the bar and patted Dan's shoulder. "We were just discussing, with your guy, the importance of romance in a relationship."

"Yeah, right." Maxine glanced at her watch. "Come on, babe, we better get going—grab the food and come on! I have to be to work."

"Yeah, babe, you better get going," Jocko mocked.

Red cracked an imaginary whip on the air and added an appropriate *thwack* sound effect.

Dan climbed off his stool. "I hate both you guys."

"But I'm your best friend," Red pointed out.

"Yeah, I wish I could take that back," Dan said.

Chapter Six

When Dan Coast followed Maxine through the front doors of the Lower Keys Behavioral Health Center where he had done his court-ordered stint, the porcine woman sitting behind the reception desk looked up and smiled. "Hi, Dan, Hi, Maxine," she said.

"How ya doin, Speranza?" Dan asked. Maxine, who was a nurse at the facility, smiled and gave a little wave.

"I'm goot, Meester Coast. How are you?"

"Wonderful!" Dan replied.

Speranza noticed the bag Dan was carrying and asked, "What dit you bring me today?"

"Sorry, Speranza, nothing for you today. It's just a cheeseburger and fries for Officer Mel's lunch.

"I like cheeseburgers, too," she sulked.

"I'll keep that in mind next time."

Dan and Maxine stepped on to the elevator and pushed the button for the third floor.

"Should I be worried about you and Speranza?" Maxine asked as the doors slid shut.

"Probably," Dan answered. "I've always had a fetish for sixty-year-old, three hundred pound Hispanic women with triple D breasts."

"That's a lot of lovin'."

"And handy too. Just think, if my hammock ever broke I could stretch one of her bras between two palm trees and problem solved."

Maxine looked up at Dan. "How come you didn't mention anything to Red about the dead guy on the beach?"

"I was about to tell him when you went to the ladies' room, but then he started talking about some guy who had stopped in to see me."

"Who?"

"He didn't know. I have to stop over later."

"Be careful."

Dan flashed a crooked grin. "Where's the fun in that?"

The doors slid open and the two walked onto the floor. Dan looked around for Dr. Richards. Richards had tried to have Dan barred from the hospital and was still pissed that Dan was able to secure his visitation rights through a large donation to the hospital. Dan still remembered the look on Richards' red face the day members of the hospital board unanimously voted to name the common room on the third floor *The Dan Coast Room*. Under normal circumstances, Dan would have declined the honor out of modesty, but knowing what it would do to Richards every time he read the gold plaque on the wall over the seventy-two inch, high definition television set that he had purchased, he agreed that *The Dan Coast Room* sounded pretty good.

Maxine swiped the name tag that hung from the lanyard around her neck and walked behind the nurse's station. Dan kept going down the hall and into the common room, He scanned the room for Mel but didn't see him. Dan did spot some other familiar faces, however. Hairy Mary sat on the sofa in front of the TV, Lucy Fenton sat next to her. "Ladies," Dan said as he walked behind the sofa toward the hall that led to Mel's room.

Lucy and Mary both turned their heads. "Hey, Danny," Mary called out. "What ya got there?"

"Lunch for Mel."

"Danny, remember that time you and I robbed that McDonald's up in Gainesville?" Mary asked, remembering something that had never happened. Mary had traumatic brain injury as the result of being thrown from a moving car by her pimp. She could easily recall things that happened in her past, but would inject people she now knew into those memories. "Holy shit! The look on those kids faces when you pulled out that .45. Remember, Danny?"

"That was one hell of a day, Mary, one hell of a day," Dan hollered back. Dr. Richards had told Dan on many occasions not to humor Mary, but he didn't listen.

When Dan got to Mel's door he peeked into the room. "Somebody order a cheeseburger and fries?" he asked, waving the bag in front of him.

Mel was sitting on his bed listening to the scanner Dan had bought him a month earlier for his birthday. Mel's eyes lit up when he saw his friend. "Hey, Dan! What's going on?"

"Picked you up a burger and fries at Red's." Dan sat the bag down on the nightstand.

Mel looked at the bag. "Did you bring me a water?"

"I forgot it in the car. Fill up your cup in lavatory."

"But Dan, I told you: The water here is tainted. Full of drugs. If I drink it, they'll be able to read my thoughts!"

Dan played along. "Right. But bottled water should be okay."

Mel sat deep in thought. "I guess so."

"Good."

Dan walked over to the small refrigerator that sat on Mel's dresser, opened it, and took out a bottle of water. He grabbed a Pepsi for himself.

Mel reached over and turned down his scanner, then grabbed the bag of food and set it on the bed between his legs. "So, what are you working on? Got a big case you need help on? Remember, I am a police officer," he said tapping the cardboard badge that hung around his neck.

Dan slid a chair over next to the bed and sat down. "Wait till you hear what happened to me this morning."

Mel took a bite of his burger. "Should I close the door? Is it top secret?"

"No, Mel, you can leave the door open."

"Okay, go."

"Well, I went down to the beach—"

"Wait!" Mel shoved a handful of fries into his mouth. "Okay, now start."

Dan rolled his eyes and took a drink of his soda. "Are you sure you're ready?"

"Yes."

"So, like I was saying, I went down to the beach this morning for a swim. While I was out there I noticed Buddy—"

"Your dog," Mel interrupted.

"Yeah, Mel, my dog. I noticed he was digging in the sand."

"Buried treasure!" Mel hollered. "There's a lot of buried treasure in these parts."

Dan took another sip of his soda. "No, not buried treasure. It was a body."

"In a treasure chest."

"There was no treasure chest, for Chrissakes. Will you just shut up and listen?"

"Sorry, go ahead."

"It was a dead body in the sand. I called Rick and told him about it, but when the police showed up, the body was—"

"Alive again!" Mel shouted. "Zombies!"

"Nope. The body was gone."

"Where did it go?"

"I have no idea," Dan answered.

Mel grinned. "And now you're working on *The Case of the Missing Body.*"

"Sure. I guess."

"Or wait—how about *The Case of the Body That Wasn't There*? I think *The Missing Body* one was a Hardy Boys mystery."

"Quick thinking, Mel, we wouldn't want to use a title that's already been done," He screwed the lid back on his Pepsi. "Well, I better get going. Enjoy the rest of your lunch."

"Okay, Dan, thanks for stopping in. If you need any help on this case, let me know."

"Will do," Dan assured him, and headed for the door.

Chapter Seven

It was a little before six when Dan walked back through the door of Red's Bar and Grill. He paused and looked around the room as the door swung shut behind him. The bar was almost empty. A man and woman sat at a four-top table to his left and another man sat at the bar sipping a beer. Red stood behind the bar polishing a glass. He made eye contact with Dan and then cocked his head toward the stranger at the bar.

Dan made his way across the room and took a seat four stools down from the guy. Red already had the tequila, Seven, and lime sitting on the bar when Dan arrived. Dan took a big swig of his drink and then looked over at the man. "Jesus Christ!" he shouted, his drink spraying from his mouth and nose. He reached for Reds bar rag as he choked. Every hair on Dan's arm and the back of his neck stood on end.

"What the hell is wrong with you?" Red asked. "You look like you've seen a ghost."

Dan was still coughing and couldn't get out the words

but pointed at the stranger.

"What?" Red asked.

"It's him!" Dan spluttered.

The unknown man was already staring at Dan with a confused look on his face. "Are you okay, pal?" he asked.

Dan had recovered from his coughing jag but could only repeat, "It's you!"

"Yeah," Red agreed. "It's him, the guy I said was in here looking for you."

"You're Dan Coast?" the man asked.

Dan shook his head yes. "And *you're* the dead guy I found this morning."

The man lowered his brow. "Dead guy?"

Dan downed the last of his drink and slid the empty glass back to Red. "Yeah. This morning, I found a dead man buried in the sand at the beach behind my house. When the police arrived, you were gone."

"Well it obviously wasn't him," Red pointed out. "He's pretty much alive."

"The deceased man looked just like me?" the stranger asked.

"Yes. Exactly like you, only bluer ... and deader."

"Oh my God," the man whispered, dropping his head and staring into the bar. "It must have been my brother."

Red pushed Dan's refilled glass back in front of him.

"Your brother?" Dan asked confusedly.

"He's been missing for a week. That's why I'm here. I came down here to find him."

"And who are *you*?" Dan asked.

The guy reached out his hand. "The names Walter Bowman."

Dan hesitantly shook the man's hand. "Dan Coast ... but you already know that, apparently."

Red shoved his arm over the bar. "Red Baxter."

"Red said you were in here earlier to see me."

"That's right. I was going to hire you to find my brother."

Dan sipped his tequila. "Well, that was easy. I'll send you a bill." Dan returned his attention to Red. "How about a plate of those Buffalo shrimp and a side of fries?"

Walter Bowman lowered his brow and stared down the bar at Dan in disbelief.

Red glanced over at Bowman and shrugged.

"But I still need your help," Bowman muttered.

Dan didn't make eye contact with Bowman but instead spoke to Red. "Ya see that, Red? Repeat costumer. I did such a great job finding his brother, now he wants to hire me again. Ya do a good job at a decent price and they come back every time."

Red smirked but said nothing. Dan could be a grade A prick, but that was part of his charm.

Bowman swiveled his stool toward Dan and leaned his elbow on the bar. "What's your problem, man?"

"Ugh," Dan said with a sigh and looked toward the ceiling in deep thought. "I'm an alcoholic, I have commitment issues, I've been told I'm quite the smart ass, I'm childish, and my last girlfriend said that I suffer from chronic grief and I carry too much baggage. I don't even know if chronic grief is a real thing, but hey, I'm not the amateur psychologist that every other person in my fucking life pretends to be. Why do you ask?"

"Are you going to help me or not?" Bowman asked.

"I just gave you a list of only half the shit that's wrong with me and you still want to hire me?"

"Yes."

"Okay, then, I guess that begs the question: What's wrong with you."

"Mr. Coast, I've asked around and I've been told you are the best at doing what I need done."

"So what you're saying is, you want to hire me to drink a bottle of tequila?"

Red laughed out loud.

Bowman shook his head and there was almost a sign of a grin. "Can you be serious for one minute?"

"Probably not, but I'll give it a shot."

"I need you to find someone else for me."

Dan cocked his head. "Exactly how many people are you missing?"

Bowman let out a sigh. "I'll start from the beginning."

"You do that, and if at any point during your story it appears as though I'm not paying attention or I'm uninterested, you just keep on talking, because Red is paying attention and he can fill me in on anything I may have missed."

Red nodded in agreement. "I'm listening," he said. "You just start from the beginning, pal."

Bowman watched as Dan downed the last of his second drink and then began his story. "My mother passed away two weeks ago in an automobile accident."

Dan threw up his hand. "Wait, let me get another

drink, this sounds sad." He sat the empty glass in front of Red and Red made him another. "Go ahead."

"As I was saying, my mother passed away in an automobile accident two weeks ago. My father, who was driving, is now on life support. The prognosis is not good."

Dan sat sipping his tequila while listening intently … and wondering how long it would be until his Buffalo shrimp arrived.

"While my brother and I were in our father's office earlier this week, going through various documents, we discovered that we have a sister."

"Order up!" Jocko hollered from the kitchen.

Red spun on his heels and disappeared through the wooden double doors that separated the bar from the kitchen.

Bowman sat silently for a second wondering if he should continue without Red.

Dan waved his hand in a circular motion. "Keep going, Bowman."

Bowman cleared his throat. "Our sister would be around twenty-five or twenty-six years old now and she lives somewhere here in Key West."

"A name?" Dan asked.

"We—that is, I—only know her first name: Angela."

"Shouldn't be too difficult. Now, let's get back to the brother."

Bowman quickly saddened. "Yes … my brother," he said, somberly. "He came down a few days ago to find our sister."

"A few days ago?"

"Wednesday."

Red walked back through the doors and sat the plate of shrimp in front of Dan.

"Fork?" Dan asked.

"You eat them with your fingers," Red said.

"Blue cheese?"

Red rolled his eyes and returned to the kitchen.

"How is it you didn't know about a sister until recently?"

"Our father did a lot of business down here back in the nineties. He owned some property. He was also part owner of a small hotel. I'm not sure which one. He traveled down here about once a month for a few years."

"And he knocked up some broad down here and had a kid," Dan added, mater-of-factly.

"Long story short, yes."

Red returned with a small plastic cup of blue cheese dressing and placed it next to the plate of shrimp. "Anything else, your majesty?"

"Mayonnaise for my fries?" Dan asked, as he animatedly looked around the bar for the condiments.

Red muttered an obscenity under his breath and went back into the kitchen.

Dan returned his attention to Bowman. "Good help is hard to find these days," he said, and shoved a blue cheese-coated shrimp into his mouth. "Go ahead with your story."

"Where was I?" Bowman asked.

"Your mom had quit giving it up so your dad was coming down to Key West once a month to bang some broad."

"Yeah ... I don't remember saying anything about my mother, Coast."

"It was implied. Moving along." Dan waved his hand.

"Any way, when my mother found out, she asked my father for a divorce. My father had nothing when they met."

"And he wasn't about to give half of what he now had away."

"Correct. So as far as we know, he never set foot in the Keys again."

"Let me help you move this story along. Now your dad is about to kick the bucket and there's a lot of money up for grabs and you want to find this sister of yours because you're a wonderful brother and you want to make sure she gets half of dear old dad's money—which would have only been a third—but you were both lucky enough to have one of your siblings get killed."

Bowman couldn't believe his ears. "I don't think 'lucky' is the word for what has happened."

"Not for your brother, anyway."

Red sat a cup of mayonnaise in front of Dan and shot him an I-dare-you-to-ask-for-anything-else look.

"Will you help me?" said Bowman. His voice held a pleading note.

"Sure, but I get paid a thousand up front and the rest when she's found. None of this waiting until the estate is settled bullshit."

Bowman pulled a checkbook from his back pocket. "Make this out to you?"

Dan dipped a fry into the mayo. "Put the checkbook back in your pocket. We'll hit the ATM on our way."

47

"On our way where?" Bowman asked.

"The police station." Dan pushed his empty plate across the bar. "I can't wait to see the look on Carver's face when he finds out I wasn't imagining the dead guy on the beach."

Chapter Eight

Dan barged into Chief Rick Carver's office without knocking. Carver was halfway through a submarine sandwich. A small bag of sour cream and onion potato chips and a Diet Coke sat to his right. He gave Dan the can't-you-knock look and sat the sandwich down on his desk.

"What now?" Carver grumbled, leaning back in his chair. His navy blue shirt was stretched across his belly and the buttons were screaming, "For the love of Christ, please, no more!"

Dan stepped aside and imitating a *The Price Is Right* model with a dramatic flip of his hand, he revealed his new client.

Carver wasn't impressed. "Who's this?"

"Walter Bowman."

Bowman nodded. "Chief."

"Is that name supposed to mean something to me?" Carver asked.

"His brother is the man I found dead on the beach this morning," Dan said.

"Wow Coast, you're turning into one hell of an illegal unlicensed private investigator." Carver looked at his watch. "It only took you about seven hours to find him."

"I didn't find him, he found me."

"That makes more sense." Carver slid his sandwich to the side. "What's the brother's name?"

"I have no idea," Dan responded, and turned to Bowman.

"His name is—or was—Warren Bowman."

"Walter and Warren Bowman," Carver said to no one in particular, and then jotted the two names down on a yellow legal pad.

"We were twins," Bowman stated.

Carver dropped the pen on the pad. "This might seem like a stupid question, Bowman, but do you know where your brother is now?"

Bowman shook his head. "No. Sorry."

"Yeah, that would have been too easy. Do you know how he ended up dead on the beach?"

Bowman again shook his head no.

"He came down here to look for their sister," Dan threw in.

Carver turned to Dan. "If I have any questions for you I'll let you know. Until then keep it zipped."

"Okey doke."

Carver returned his attention to Bowman. "When was the last time you saw your brother?"

"Wednesday morning. I drove him to the airport, he

boarded the plane, and that's the last time I saw him."

"What airport?"

"Sea-Tac ... Seattle."

Carver jotted it down. "Did you hear from him at all while he was here?"

"No, not a word."

"How long are you going to be in town?"

"A few days, I guess, until I find our sister."

Carver rubbed his face with a beefy paw in exasperation.

"You look just like Brian Keith in Family Affair when you do that, Rick" Dan observed.

"Shut up, Coast!" Rick boomed. "Okay, Bowman, now what is this about a sister?"

"Warren and I recently found out that we have a sister. According to documentation we found in Dad's office, she lives in Key West."

"A name?"

"No last name, but her first name is Angela."

"Might she have you and your father's last name?"

"She could, I guess."

Dan spoke up. "I was going to ask if you could run her name to see if anything came up."

Carver pressed a button on his phone. "Donna can you check with DMV on an Angela Bowman?"

A voice came from the speaker. "Coming right up, Chief."

"You have a number where I can reach you while you're in town?" Carver asked.

Bowman gave him his cell number and Carver wrote it at the top of the page next to where he had written Bowman's name.

"Chief," Donna said.

"Yeah."

"We got an Angela Bowman, eighty-three years old, 2-9-4-1-7 Saratoga Avenue, on Big Pine Key."

"Thanks, Donna," Carver said. "Probably not her." He jabbed the intercom button on the phone with the finger of one hand while reaching for his sandwich with the other. "Now, if you two gentlemen will excuse me, I would like to get back to my lunch."

Dan reached back, turned the door knob, and pushed the door open. "You'll let us know if you find anything?" he asked.

Rick raised his eye brow and paused mid-chew. "Oh, sure, we'll let you know. We might even give you a call if we just want to talk or if we need your advice on how to do our jobs."

Dan said, "Um, thanks, Rick," and went out the door.

As the two men walked back through the station toward the door, Bowman turned to Dan. "He's not going to let us know anything, is he?"

"Very perceptive, Bowman. We won't hear from him again until he has questions for one of us."

"He's kind of a dick."

"Ya think?"

Bowman pushed the door open and let Dan exit first. "So what's next?"

"We'll have someone search hospital records and see if your old man was listed as the father on any birth certificates back in the nineties."

Bowman grinned. "It's just like on TV. You PIs always have contacts and informants to find out information for you."

"Yeah, just like on TV," Dan grumbled as he climbed into the passenger seat of Bowman's rental, a black Lincoln Town Car.

Bowman's eyes shone with eagerness. "Who's your contact at the hospital, someone you helped once on a big case, someone's life you saved in a shootout?" he asked excitedly.

"Down, boy. It's just my girlfriend."

Chapter Nine

It was almost six-thirty when Dan told Walter Bowman to "Take the next left." Bowman did as he was asked and the two made their way down Twelfth Street toward the Lower Keys Behavior Health Center. Bowman drove for another five blocks and Dan said, "You can pull in right here, and park in that space that says RESERVED FOR DAN COAST.

Bowman looked puzzled as he parked and shut off the engine. "You have your own parking space?"

"Yup. The bigger the donation, the closer to the front door," Dan explained as he climbed from the car.

Bowman stood, shut the car door, and looked around the parking lot. "Yours is the furthest reserved spot from the door," he pointed out.

"Yeah," Dan agreed as he made his way through the automatic doors. "No need to show off. It was just to prove a point."

Dan and Bowman walked past the front desk. "Back

so soon, Meester Coast?" Speranza asked.

"I just can't stay away, Speranza," Dan returned.

The two men walked onto the elevator, the doors shut, and when they reopened Dan was staring down the familiar hall of floor number three.

When they stepped off the elevator and into the hallway Maxine looked up from the desk and smiled. "Back so soon?"

"That's what Speranza said," Dan replied. He walked up to the desk and leaned in for a kiss.

Maxine instinctively looked around the floor for Dr. Richards. Not spying him, she quickly pecked Dan on the lips.

Dan made introductions and added, "Walter's looking for his sister."

Maxine furrowed her brow. "It seems like we've been down this road before," she joked, referring to Dan's last case, in which Officer Mel's sister went missing. "I don't have her this time."

Bowman cocked his head. "I don't understand."

"It's a long story," Dan assured him.

"How can I help?" Maxine asked.

"I was wondering if you could search back through Monroe County birth records from here, and see if you can find a baby girl that would have been born sometime in the early nineties," Dan explained. "Her first name is Angela. Not sure about a last name, may have been Bowman. The father might have been listed as—" Dan glanced over at Bowman for the answer.

"Kent … Kent Bowman."

Maxine turned and walked to a computer that sat on a

desk behind the nurses station. "Hold on," she said, and began punching some keys.

"Maxine, is there a problem here?" came a voice from behind them that Dan instantly recognized.

Maxine quickly cleared the screen.

Dan turned to see Dr. Richards approaching.

"No, Dr. Richards, there's no problem," Maxine answered. "Dan is just here to see Mel."

Richards walked up to the group and leaned his elbow on the counter. "Weren't you already here once today, Mr. Coast?" he asked.

"Is there a limit, Sigmund, to how many times a day I can visit?"

Richards took a deep breath. "No. there's not a limit … and I thought we agreed that it was Dr. Richards from now on, not Sigmund."

"Oops! Old habits, Doc."

Richards glanced at his watch. "Maxine, I believe it is time to start meds."

"Just getting ready to start that, Dr. Richards."

"Um-hum," Richards turned and made his way back toward his office.

Maxine shot Dan a dirty look. "How many times do you think you can get me into trouble before he fires me?"

"He can't fire you," Dan said.

"No, but he can make someone else do it. Now you two go visit Mel for a minute so he doesn't think I was lying."

"Fine," Dan said as he turned. "Come on Bowman, you'll get a kick out of this guy."

Bowman followed. "Can't wait! I've met so many interesting characters so far today. By the way, what was that Sigmund business?"

"Sigmund and the Sea Monsters. The old Saturday morning TV show. Doesn't Richards' mop of seaweed hair remind you of Sigmund?"

Bowman blinked in glassy-eyed incomprehension.

"Never mind."

Dan knocked on Mel's open door.

Mel turned and saw Dan and Bowman. "Business or pleasure?" Mel asked.

Dan thought for a second. "Um ... business."

Mel threw up his index finger. "Give me a sec." He walked to the television and shut it off. Then he went to his nightstand, opened the drawer and pulled out his aluminum foil-covered, cardboard badge and hung it around his neck. He looked into the mirror over his dresser and adjusted his hair with the tips of his fingers, straightened up, and puffed out his chest. "Come on in, gentlemen."

Dan stepped aside and motioned for Bowman to enter first. "Walter Bowman, this is Officer Mel Gormin. Mel, Walter Bowman."

Mel and Bowman shook hands. "It's nice to meet you, Mr. Bowman."

Bowman was confused. "It's ... nice, to meet ... you ... too?"

Mel returned to the nightstand for his note pad and pen. "What can I do for you boys, today?"

Dan spoke up. "Mr. Bowman is looking for is sister, Mel."

Mel gave a condescending chuckle. "Looking for his sister, huh?" He tossed the pad back on the nightstand. "I think we've been down this road before, Dan. What we have here is what the experts call an open and shut case. She's probably staying with Maxine."

"Maxine, the nurse?" Bowman asked.

"Not this time, Mel. Mr. Bowman came to Key West in search of a sister he has never met."

"You've never met your own sister?" Mel asked. "That's very strange."

"He never met her, Mel," Dan explained, "because he never knew she existed until recently. His father was cheating on his mother and knocked up some broad down here years ago, and never told anyone that he had a daughter."

Mel finger-drummed his lower lip reflectively. "Hmm. Your father sounds like a real piece of shit. No offense."

"None taken," Bowman said.

"Mr. Bowman also has a twin brother, Warren, who came down earlier in the week to find the sister, but we think he may have been killed."

Mel once again picked up his note pad and readied his pen. "Had you ever met your brother before?" he asked.

Bowman nodded. "Of course. We grew up together."

"I see," Mel said as he made notes on the pad. "And which one of you was the evil twin?"

"Evil twin?" Bowman asked.

"In every movie and television show there is always a good twin and an evil twin. Was your brother the good twin or the evil twin?

Bowman, glanced toward Dan, and then back to Mel. "Warren had his troubles in the past, but I wouldn't categorize him as *evil*."

"I knew it! From this point on we will be referred to your brother as"—Mel widened his eyes, made finger quotes, and did a damn good imitation of Vincent Price—"*the evil twin*."

Dan smirked at the look of total confusion on Bowman's face. "Okay then, we better get going, Mel. Come on, Bowman."

Mel closed the note pad. "I think I have everything I need to begin my investigation," he said. "I'll let you gentlemen know if I come up with anything."

Bowman backed up toward the door. "It was nice to meet you, Mel."

"You too," Mel agreed.

Dan turned and together they left the room and walked down the hall toward the elevator. Maxine was nowhere to be seen as they walked past the nurse's station, and Dan was a little disappointed that he wouldn't be able to say good-bye.

Dan pressed the down button and the elevator doors parted.

"Wow. That was educational," Bowman said.

The two men stepped onto the elevator and the doors closed behind them. "Yeah, I figured you would enjoy meeting Officer Mel. Everyone does," Dan said. "His sister turned up missing a few months ago and he asked me to look into it. Turned out some bad cops that used to work with Mel in Los Angeles were after him and his sister. His sister had gone into hiding and was staying with Maxine."

"I assume Mel is ..." Bowman hoped Dan would

finish his thought.

He did.

"Crazy? Sure, but no more so than the next guy. He's just got the papers to prove it. Plus, he's as sweet a person as you'd ever want to meet. And harmless.

The elevator doors opened and the two men came face to face with a tall, thin black man holding a mop. The man stepped aside. "Be careful there, Mr. Coast, floors wet," he said.

Dan side stepped the small puddle. "Thanks, Calvin."

Bowman maneuvered around the wet spot in the floor as well and nodded to Calvin. Calvin returned the nod and Bowman followed Dan through the front doors.

"You seem to know everyone here pretty well," Bowman commented as they reached the car. "How long have you been dating Maxine?"

"Not that long, a few months, maybe." Dan placed his palms on the roof of the car and looked over it at Bowman, who was standing on the driver's side. "I got to know everyone pretty good during my six week stay here."

Bowman was reaching for the door handle, but froze. "What do you mean, your stay here?"

"I was a patient here a few months back."

"Are you serious? A patient in a nut house?"

"Hey, Bowman, I gave you several reasons not to hire me."

"You left out, mental patient."

"Well … yeah. You might not have hired me, if you knew that one. "Wanna back out?"

Bowman mused for a moment. "No, I don't think so. This could be the most excitement I've had in … forever.

Chapter Ten

Bowman pulled the Lincoln to the curb in front of the white bungalow at 632 Beach View Street. "Here ya go," he said. "You'll call me if you hear anything?"

Dan pulled the handle and shoved open the door with his foot. "You betcha," he answered.

"Thanks. Catch ya later."

Dan pushed the door closed and Bowman drove off. Dan watched as the Town Car paused at the stop sign and swung a left onto George Street, and then he glanced over toward Edna McGee's front window. Sure enough, she was watching. No sooner than Dan raised his hand to wave than the curtain swung closed. He grinned and paused for a moment knowing what was coming next.

Edna's front door opened and onto her front porch she stepped. She lifted the top of her mailbox to search for the day's mail, and then looked across the street at Dan. "Oh … Danny, I didn't know you were home. Would you be a dear and come over? My kitchen sink faucet is dripping and I can't get it to stop."

"Sure thing, Mrs. McGee." Dan pivoted on his toes and made his way across the street.

When he reached Edna's porch she said, "Thanks, Danny, I don't know what I would do if you didn't live across the street from me."

"You'd have one hell of a water bill," Dan answered as he walked past her into the house.

Edna chuckled.

Dan could hear the water running before he even got to the kitchen. "This is a little more than a drip, Edna!" he exclaimed.

"I didn't know how to shut it off."

Dan opened the cabinet under the sink and got down on his knee. "You could have called me. I gave you my cell phone number."

Edna waved him off. "I told you, I don't know how to call those cell phones."

Dan reached under the sink and spun the shut-off until the water stopped. "Edna, you call a cell phone the same way you call a land line."

"I don't know how to use a land line either."

"Your phone *is* a land line."

"I don't think so, Danny. I'm pretty sure it's just a regular phone."

"A regular phone *is*—never mind." Dan shook his head and climbed to his feet. "I had a package of washers in my shed, I think. I'll check if they're still there and stop back by in the morning and change it."

"Thank you, Danny." Edna turned and went to the small Formica-topped, chrome-legged table that sat against the wall. She picked up a plate wrapped in aluminum foil.

"Here, Danny, I baked you a plate of brownies, no walnuts, just like you like."

Dan smiled and took the plate. "Thanks, Edna. I'll be over around ten tomorrow morning."

"I'll be here," Edna said.

Dan left Edna's house, plate in hand, and made his way back toward his own home. The sun had set and the sky was beginning to darken. When he reached the middle of the street, he paused and looked to his right. Sitting at the end of the street was a black Ford Mustang.

Shit, he thought. He squinted in an attempt to see if someone was inside, but the windows were tinted. He continued on and as he reached the path to his front door the engine started and the headlights came on.

Dan turned toward the vehicle and slowly backed toward his front steps as the Mustang drove by. He watched until it reached the corner and turned. He let out a deep breath he didn't realize he was holding. *What the Christ?*

Dan went up the steps and pushed open the screen door, walked onto his porch, and stepped over the welcome mat that read, THE COAST'S. As he walked through the front door and across the living room floor, he glanced down at the photograph of Alex that sat on the small round table next to Buddy's flannel bed. Over four years had gone by since her death. Time heals all wounds, or so the saying goes. Dan was still wondering exactly how much time that would be.

He sat the plate of brownies on the dining room table and went directly to the bar. He grabbed a glass, went to the kitchen for ice. *I should get a small ice machine to set next to the bar,* he thought. He had thought that *many* times over the last few years, and had even priced them a few times at The Restaurant Store over on Eaton Street, but just never pulled the trigger.

Dan dumped about a shot and a half of tequila into the glass and then filled it the rest of the way with 7Up. He grabbed a brownie and flipped on the back light as he went through the kitchen door. He made his way down the gravel pathway that led to the two Adirondack chairs that sat next to the fire pit, and took a seat. He bit into the brownie and then took a sip of his drink. Both had been prepared to perfection.

When Bev's back door creaked open Dan's attention went from the beach to his neighbor's back deck. Bev walked out followed by Dan's dog, Buddy.

"Are you looking for someone?" Bev called. Buddy continued down the steps and toward his own yard.

"Usually," Dan responded. "But you're probably talking about that dog."

Bev followed along behind Buddy. "You should be nicer to that dog as you so coarsely put it. He's man's best friend, you know."

"I wonder what man that is." Buddy walked up to the chair and Dan reached out and scratched his head. "You my best friend, pal?" Buddy lay down at Dan's feet seeming to ignore him. "That's what I figured."

"Want some company?" Bev asked, as she took a seat in the other Adirondack chair.

"Always," Dan replied. He rattled the ice in his empty glass. "If I didn't have company I would have to make my own drinks."

Bev shook her head, stood, and reached for Dan's glass. "You have issues."

"No kidding."

"Tequila?"

"Of course."

Bev walked up the gravel pathway and disappeared through the kitchen door.

Dan lifted his leg and rested his foot on Buddy's back. "Foot stools are man's best friend," he said.

Buddy lifted his head, shot Dan a look, and dropped his head back to the dirt.

Bev returned moments later holding two glasses. She handed one to Dan and returned to her seat. "Maxine working?"

"Yup."

"Till eleven?"

"Yup."

"What did you do all day?"

"Picked up a case today."

Bev smirked. "You're calling them cases now?"

Dan ignored the jab. "I'm helping a guy find his sister."

"Did you check Maxine's house?"

"That joke has already been used today ... twice."

"Edna said the cops were here this morning for a while."

"Yeah, they were. Where were you?"

"I went to the gym and then to pick up a few groceries."

Dan raised his brow. "The gym?"

Bev shook her head. "I knew I shouldn't have said anything."

"I thought ya looked like you've been bulking up."

"Shut up."

Dan took a sip of his drink. "Pumpin' some iron, were ya?"

Bev playfully pointed a scolding finger at her neighbor. "Shut ... up."

"Okay, okay," Dan said, throwing up his hand. "Just teasing ya, little Miss Schwarzenegger."

Bev took a drink of her tequila. "So why *were* the cops here this morning?"

"Long story short, we found a dead guy on the beach. I left a message for Carver and then we ate breakfast. By the time Carver got here the body had disappeared."

"You ate breakfast *before* you even got ahold of the cops?"

"I know, I know," Dan groaned. "I already heard it from Carver. I was hungry and hungover. Anyway, my client is the brother of the dead guy that's looking for his sister."

"Oooo, client! I love it when you talk all grown-up. I assume he's also looking for his dead brother."

"Yeah, but we went to the police station and explained everything to Carver, so he's also in on the search."

"Well I'm glad to see you two can put aside your differences and work together."

"I didn't say we were working together."

"Did you ever apologize for calling him a fat bastard in front of half the police force?"

"Yeah, several times."

"And?"

"And he's still fat."

Bev shook her head. "It's no wonder you only have three friends." She sipped her drink.

"For your information, I have five friends."

"Your dad and your girlfriend don't count."

"Okay, three," Dan agreed. "What time did you leave for fantasy camp this morning?"

"Fantasy camp?"

Dan made finger quotes. "The gym, as you call it."

"Wow! You're an asshole."

"Tell me something I don't know."

"I left a little after seven," Bev said.

"You didn't notice anyone out back … near the beach?"

"No," Bev answered. "Just my drunken neighbor and his lady friend in his hammock."

"Funny," Dan remarked, and once again rattled the ice in his glass. "Why don't you make us another drink?"

"Why don't *you* get off your lazy ass and make us another drink? Fantasy camp. What a dick."

Dan stood with a groan and grabbed Bev's glass. "Fine." He was halfway to the back door when he paused and turned around. "Hey, Bev, did you notice a black Ford Mustang on the street at all today?"

"No. Why?"

"Um … I, uh … I gotta get a new car, eventually. I saw a Mustang parked down the street earlier, thought it was kinda nice." Dan turned and headed to the house.

"I think they're douchy," Bev called out.

Chapter Eleven

Maxine sat on the edge of the bed tying her running shoes. "Why don't you come with me?"

Dan rolled over and looked at the clock on the nightstand. Seven-thirty. "I would, but I have a lot of work to do in the yard this morning."

Maxine looked over her shoulder at him. "From the looks of it, you haven't done anything in that yard since you bought the place."

"No one's asked me to go running since I bought the place."

"A little cardio might be good for your heart," Maxine informed him.

"A little cardio might stop my heart," Dan replied.

"You have an answer for everything, don't you?"

"Should I answer that?"

"Whatever." Maxine started for the bedroom door. "I have to stretch."

"Why don't you climb back in bed and we'll stretch together?"

"I would, but you have a lot of work to do in the yard."

"I knew *that* would come back to bite me in the ass." Dan swung his legs over and put his feet on the floor. He grabbed yesterday's shorts and went to the dresser for a T-shirt. He held up the shirt and read the front. OZZY OSBOURNE, NO MORE TOURS. He thought for a second. *Ninety, ninety-one?* He remembered the concert in Saratoga. His mother had given him gas money and paid for his ticket so he would take his little sister and her friend.

Dan paused and gazed into the mirror over the dresser. *Holy shit!* He thought. *I remember seeing that concert and thinking, wow, Ozzy is really old. Now I'm as old as you were then, Oz.* Dan poked at the small bags under his eyes. *Old or tired. Maybe I should have gone for a run ... naw.*

He glanced back at the clock. Seven-forty-one. *Maybe I'll just run to the kitchen and make coffee.*

As Dan exited the hall into the dining room he could already smell the coffee. *What time did she get up?* He glanced over at Buddy, sound asleep on his bed. The morning's edition of the *Key West Citizen* was lying on the table next to a file folder containing the names of babies born in Monroe County in the early nineties.

He went on into the kitchen and poured himself a cup of coffee. First he put his nose up to the cup and sniffed it, then he tasted it. *Dammit.* He looked over at the small bag of coffee that read, DUNKIN DONUTS, CARMEL COFFEE CAKE. He stared at the pot for a second, contemplating dumping the rest of it and making a fresh pot of *regular* coffee. He took another sip. *I'll get used to it ... I guess.*

*****

Dan was sitting in an Adirondack chair next to the fire pit thumbing through the papers in the file folder when Maxine jogged down the gravel path that led from the driveway to the backyard. Buddy lay on the ground next to Dan. Maxine ran past him and onto the beach.

"Good run?" he asked, as she galloped through the yard.

"Always," she replied. "You should give it a try."

Buddy jumped up, grabbed his tennis ball, and ran after her.

Dan went back to making notes on the inside cover of the folder.

When Maxine returned to the yard she was carrying her running shoes and socks. "Was there anything of any use in there?" she asked, pointing at the folder.

Buddy dropped his ball at her feet and stared at her.

"Yes. Thanks," Dan responded. "Out of all the babies born in the Keys during that time frame, eleven had no father listed on the birth certificate. But only six of those were girls."

Maxine reached down, grabbed the tennis ball, and lobbed it toward the beach. Buddy bounded down the path after it. "Well, that narrows it down quite a bit. Were any of the girls named Angela?"

"Not one of them. But two of them *were* listed as Baby Girl, with a last name."

"Baby girl? Isn't there some law that says you have to name your kid?" Dan asked.

"Not right away. It happens sometimes. Parents can't

decide on a name. They just have to have a name before you apply for their social security number."

"So, how do we find out the girls' names?"

"The mothers' full names are listed next to each child. You'll probably have to ask Rick for help."

Dan shook his head. "No way. Red has a friend that works at Motor Vehicle. Maybe he can help us out. He's been pretty useful in the past. I'll give Red a call later."

"After the yard work?"

"Yeah, probably won't get to that today."

"I didn't think so. I'm going to jump in the shower. I'll make some breakfast in a bit." Maxine turned and started for the house.

"Good, I'm starving."

She stopped and turned around. "You couldn't be *too* hungry, or you would have had breakfast ready when I got back from my run."

"Yeah, you're right," Dan agreed. "I guess I'm not really *that* hungry."

Maxine shook her head. "What did you do before I came along?" she asked.

"I went *out* for breakfast."

"You know what? That's a good idea." Maxine said. "I'll be ready in twenty minutes."

What the Christ?

Chapter Twelve

As Dan and Maxine got to the bottom of the steps, Dan held out his hand.

"What?" Maxine asked.

"Keys," Dan replied.

Maxine rolled her eyes. "What's the matter, hon, does it emasculate you when I drive the car?"

"No. it just makes me feel like less of a man. Now give me the keys."

"Yeah, well, too bad. I'm driving, so get in the car. Besides, you don't get your license back for another two weeks."

Dan climbed into the passenger seat and shut the door of Maxine's blue, 2013 Ford Focus. "I can drive just as good without a license as I could when I had a license," Dan informed her.

"Oh, so you can get just as drunk, lead police on a high speed chase, and smash through a concrete wall just as good without a license. Good to know." Maxine put the car in reverse and backed out of the driveway and into the street.

Dan glanced over to see Mrs. MacGee standing on her front porch. *Shit!* "Stop the car and pull over," he said.

"What's the matter?"

"I told Edna I'd fix her faucet this morning. Let me go over and tell her I'll do it after breakfast."

Maxine pulled to the curb and put the car in park and also got out.

"Morning, Edna," Maxine called out.

"Morning, dear," Edna called back.

"We're headed for breakfast," Maxine said. "Would you care to join us?"

What the Christ? Dan shot Maxine a look of complete terror.

"I already ate dear, but thanks for the offer."

Thank God, Dan thought. "Oh, that's too bad," he said.

"Maybe next time," Edna said. "How was your run this morning, dear? You were up bright and early."

"It was a really nice run. Perfect temperature for it."

"How far do you run?"

"I think I did about eight miles this morning."

Edna placed her hand on her chest. "Oh my goodness, that's so far!"

Dan waited for a break in the conversation and jumped in. "Edna, I'll be right over after we get back from breakfast to fix that faucet. All right?"

"That's fine, Danny. I was just hoping I could take a shower this morning."

"Edna, you can take a shower. I only shut off the *kitchen* faucet," Dan explained. "You can still use the bathroom and shower."

"Oh, well, I think I'll wait just the same. I don't want to mess something up."

"Edna, you can't mess some—Good idea, just wait till I fix it."

"Okay, Danny. Thanks." Edna MacGee turned and went back into her house.

"Wow," Dan said as he turned and made his way back to the car.

"Be nice," Maxine scolded him.

The two of them climbed back into the car and Maxine pulled the shifter into drive.

"How was your run, dear?" Dan said, mocking Mrs. McGee in a crotchety voice.

"Stop it! You know she's good to you, Dan. She's sweet, and she dotes on you like a grandmother."

"Yeah, well she can be a pest, and I think she's showing signs of Alzheimer's."

"Alzheimer's? Very good! A little surprised you didn't say old-timer's."

"I'm not a moron, Maxine."

"I know you're not, Dan. Sometimes, though, I think you want people to *believe* that you are. You know what I think?"

"No, but you'll tell me anyway."

"You're a softie pretending to be a tough guy. And

somewhere under that cynical veneer there beats the heart of a poet."

More damn armchair psychology. Dan quickly changed the subject. "Well, anyway, I'm surprised the old biddy didn't already know the route you ran."

"You're lucky you have neighbors who watch what's going on in the neighborhood. Besides, I think I'll be changing my route anyway."

"Why's that?"

"Some guy kept driving by me this morning, gawking," Maxine said.

"*Kept* driving by. How many times?" Dan asked.

Maxine took a right on to White Street. "Two or three times."

"What kind of car?"

"It was black. A Mustang, I think."

"Which was it, two, or three?"

Maxine thought for a second. "Three, I think."

"Did he say anything?"

"No. He just drove by real slow each time and stared at me. It was kinda creepy." She took a left at Truman Avenue.

"What direction was he heading the last time you saw him?"

"West. I think I was on Flagler."

Dan pointed at the next intersection. "Take a left up here. Let's run by Red's quick."

"It's Sunday," Maxine pointed out. "Is something wrong?"

"I hope not; my gut instinct says to make sure he'll be there. He goes in every Sunday morning to clean."

Maxine swung another left onto Grinnell Street.

*****

Maxine drove the Focus into the parking lot of Red's Bar and Grill.

"Stop right here," Dan said.

She came to a stop in the middle of the parking lot, parallel to the front of the building, and put the car in park. She could see the concern on Dan's face. "Are you sure everything is okay? You're starting to worry me."

Dan opened the door. "Just wait in the car, I'll be right out." The stones underneath his feet crunched as he moved swiftly, but cautiously, toward the entrance door. He felt the vibration of his phone. He paused and pulled the cell from his pocket and looked at the screen. It was Red.

"Hello?"

"Where are you?"

"In your parking lot. Where are you?" Dan scanned the front of the building as he stood motionless in the parking lot, like a man in the middle of a mine field.

"Laying on the floor."

"What's going on?" Maxine whispered out the window.

Dan gave her a "Shh!"

"Sorry!" she whispered back.

"Why are you lying on the floor, Red?"

"I threw out my back."

"Is it safe to come in?"

"Yup."

Dan turned back to Maxine. "Come on."

"Yes, *sir*," Maxine responded, and climbed out of the vehicle. The two of them walked up to the front of the building.

Dan pushed open the door and went in first. The lights were off but the sun coming through the door and windows provided plenty of light. The room smelled of stale cigarettes and booze. Ashtrays on the tables hadn't been emptied yet and last night's beer bottles and glasses lined the bar. A couple bottles near the middle of the bar were lying on their sides and a bottle was smashed on the floor. Dan glanced over at the old Wurlitzer juke box to his left. Half of a bar stool was sticking out of the front of it. *That's a shame*, Dan thought.

"Looks like a hurricane hit the place," Maxine observed.

Dan smirked. "How original. Red … Red, where are you?"

"Behind the bar!" The voice was at once weak and surly.

Dan walked around to the end of the bar and looked behind it. Red lay on his back, his arms at his side. A blood trail from his nose ran to his top lip and then down his cheek toward the floor. A red welt was beginning to swell next to his right eye. His blue and white Hawaiian shirt was ripped and beer soaked and one leg of his beige cargo shorts was stained with blood.

"Watcha doin' there, buddy?" Dan asked.

"Just layin' here," Red responded. "Thinking."

"What are ya thinking about?"

"How much I hate you."

"Black Mustang?" Dan asked.

"Good guess."

Dan moved closer and stuck out his hand.

Maxine climbed up on a bar stool, and kneeling on the seat she peeked over the bar at Red. "Should we call and ambulance?" she asked.

"Nope," Red answered, and grabbed Dan's hand. He winced in pain and let out a couple whimpers. He breathed in through his clenched teeth and at one point even made a sound like a small dog yelping.

Dan helped him around to the front of the bar and onto a bar stool. Maxine went around to the bar sink and ran cold water over a hand towel. Then she scooped some ice out of the ice maker, wrapped it up in the towel, and handed it to Dan. Red took the ice-filled towel and placed in against his eye.

"What happened?" Maxine asked.

"First things first. Somebody fix me a drink," Red grumbled.

"Coming right up," Dan said.

"Lover boy from Friday evening's pool party showed up with two friends," Red explained. "They wanted to know where the camera was and if anyone else had seen the photographs."

Dan poured a double shot of Scotch over a rocks glass filled with ice and slid it across the bar to Red. "What did you tell them?"

"I told them the truth. I didn't have the camera, and I

had no idea if anyone else had seen the pictures."

"Huh," Dan said. "This guy followed Maxine on her run this morning, and he was parked in his car on my street last night. Sounds like he doesn't want anyone to see the photographs of his private swim lessons with Mrs. Hamilton."

"And it sounds like he doesn't care what he has to do to get them back," Maxine added. She pointed at Red. "This could have been me this morning."

"Yeah, but we both know who it should have been," Red said, glaring at Dan.

"Sorry!" said Dan. "I wasn't supposed to give the photos to Hamilton until Tuesday evening. Maybe I better give him a call today and find out what's going on."

Red downed the last of his Scotch. "Maybe you better."

"What about Walter Bowman?" Maxine asked.

"Christ!" Dan said. "Don't ever let me take on two things at once again. This is too confusing. Now I need a drink."

"I'm hungry," Maxine announced. "I need breakfast. You can have one drink."

Red made the sound of a whip being cracked and then chuckled. "One drink, Danny boy!"

'Okay, that's getting old."

Chapter Thirteen

After breakfast and a quick stop by the grocery store Dan and Maxine returned home. Charles Hamilton didn't answer his cell so Dan left a message for him to call back. Walter Bowman did answer his phone so Dan asked him if he could meet him at Red's a few minutes after three.

Dan had searched his shed and found a pack of assorted washers. It only took about thirty minutes to fix Mrs. MaGee's kitchen faucet. Now she could shower, do her laundry, and whatever else million-year-old ladies did with water on a daily basis. Edna thanked Dan and promised that a fresh baked batch of oatmeal-chocolate chip cookies, Dan's favorite, would soon be on its way over.

With chores done, except for yard work, Dan had made himself a drink and was now sitting in one of the Adirondack chairs near the fire pit. His drink half gone, he sat doing the word jumble. Buddy lay at his feet. Seagulls bounced around on the beach searching for bits of potato chip thrown to them by a young boy walking by with his mother.

Dan looked up and closed his eyes. He felt the warmth of the sun on his face and for one split second he remembered why he had moved here. His thoughts went quickly to his wife, Alex. The only thing his lottery winnings couldn't buy him was the only thing he wanted, for Alex to be sitting next to him in the chair that was meant for her. He drifted off to sleep and dreamed of a time when life was perfect.

*****

Dan was startled awake by the ringing of his cell phone. He jumped, spilling the watered-down drink on his shorts. He fumbled for his phone. "Hello?"

Buddy raised his head and shot Dan a judgmental look, scratched the side of his face with his front paw, and then rested his chin on Dan's foot.

"Coast? It's Charles Hamilton. I had a message you called."

Dan stood and walked toward the beach as he talked. "Yeah, I called. That guy you had me take pictures of, playing naked footsie with your wife, tracked down a friend of mine and kicked the shit out of him this morning. He's also been watching my house for the last two day."

"I'm sorry to hear that. Is your friend okay?"

"He's a tough guy, but like I said, they beat the shit out of him. And now this douche is watching my house. This job was supposed to be taking a few photos for five hundred bucks. Now it's turning into something a lot more dicey."

"Don't worry, Mr. Coast, I'll reimburse your friend

for any pain and suffering, and you, as well, for any inconvenience this may have caused."

"It's not the money, Hamilton. I just want to know what this psycho is capable of."

"Clement's a nobody, Coast. He's just a bothersome piece of shit on my shoe. I'm surprised it even went this far."

"Clement?" Dan asked. "When you hired me you made out that you didn't know the kid."

"I may not have been completely honest with you. I knew his name. I found some text messages on my wife's cell phone, and I had a cop friend of mine run the number."

"So what did you need me for?"

"Proof. Those photographs are my way out. Our prenup says that if she's having an affair she gets nothing. Coast, those pictures are worth about eight million dollars to her, and there's no telling how much she offered Clement to get them back."

"That's just great, Hamilton. You hired me for five hundred bucks to take pictures worth eight million."

"Hey, you quoted *me* the price. Coast, you guard those photographs with your life and I promise you I'll make it worth your while." Hamilton hung up the phone without waiting for Dan to respond.

"Let's hope so," Dan whispered. "It's not just me I'm worried about." He hung up his phone and slid it back into his pocket.

The young boy with the bag of potato chips was walking by again with his mom and pointed at Dan. "Look, Mommy, that man peed his pants."

Dan looked down at the wet spot on his shorts. *What the Christ!*

.

Chapter Fourteen

At two-thirty Maxine left for work. Dan watched through the front door as she backed out of the driveway and made her way down the street. He turned and went into the bedroom and opened the closet door. Getting down on his knees, he grabbed the two pairs of Maxine's shoes that sat on the closet floor and moved them aside. He pulled back the carpet and removed the two loose floorboards to reveal a secret earthen compartment under the house that had become quite useful for hiding things. Dan felt around in the darkness below and grabbed the small black bag he kept there. He pulled it out, sat it on the floor next to him, and unzipped it.

Inside the bag, among other things, was a lot of cash. Dan thought back to Tim Garvey who had once faked his own death and hired Dan to find his wife, Tess, who had stolen the life insurance money and taken off with her boyfriend, Jeff Hinder. Dan found the wife and in the end, also found the money. With everyone who knew about the money ending up dead, Dan assumed ownership of the cash. He returned a large portion of the money to Owen

Reeves, its rightful owner. Then, after paying himself what Tim Garvey owed him—along with a very generous donation to the Lower Keys Behavioral Center—eight hundred thousand dollars had dwindled down to a little less than three hundred K.

Dan wasn't after the money in the bag. He was after the Beretta 92FS 9mm Inox that he had taken from Jimmy P, a mobster he had killed. Dan wrapped his fingers around the grip and pulled the chrome weapon from the bag. He felt the weight of it in his hand. He turned the gun and read the engraving on the barrel: *Buon Compleanno Figlio Mio*. Dan didn't know Italian, but Jimmy P had told him the gun was a gift from his father and the inscription said Happy Birthday My Son.

Cash taken from a dead man, a gun taken from a dead man. Dan wondered what he would confiscate next.

Dan sat the gun on the floor next to Maxine's shoes, pulled open the bag, and looked inside. Lying on top of the money was a photograph of Candi with an "I", a woman he had met at a BBQ joint in Miami. He dated Candi for a while but it takes a special kind of woman to have a lasting relationship with an immature alcoholic with commitment issues. Next to the photo of Candi was another picture. It was a selfie of himself and a young girl named Paula he had once tried to protect from her abusive husband. He didn't try hard enough and Paula was soon murdered by her husband, Jimmy P.

When Dan was finished with his stroll down memory lane he zipped up the bag and tossed it back in the hole. He grabbed his camera off of the nightstand and placed *it* in the hole, on top of the bag, put the floor boards and carpet back, and picked up the 9mm. He released the clip, checked it for shells, and then jammed the magazine back into the grip. He pulled open the nightstand drawer on his side of the bed and placed the gun inside for quick retrieval. He stared at the nightstand for a second and then removed the pistol from the drawer, placed it on the floor, and slid it under the nightstand with his foot. He stepped back to see if the weapon could be seen. He was satisfied it couldn't.

A car pulled up out front and Dan looked out the bedroom window. It was Walter Bowman. *Christ!* Dan thought. *I told him to meet me at Red's.*

Dan slid the nightstand drawer closed and went to meet Walter Bowman at the front door. When he got there, Bowman already had his face pressed against the glass. When he saw Dan coming he stepped back.

"You make one shitty peeping Tom," Dan informed him, as he opened the door.

"I wasn't sure if you were here," Bowman said.

"Why are *you* here?" Dan asked.

"I remembered hearing you say that you didn't have a car, so I thought I would just swing by here."

"Good thinking."

Bowman walked in and looked around the house. "Nice place," he said. "How many rooms are upstairs?"

Dan turned and made his way into the dining room and to the bar. "There are no rooms upstairs; what ya see is what ya get. You want a drink, Bowman?"

"Sure. Irish whiskey, if ya got it."

"I don't."

"Anything's fine, then."

Dan made himself a tequila and 7Up, and since anything was fine he also made one for Bowman. He handed Bowman his drink and then motioned toward the file folder on the table. "Maxine narrowed our search down to three names. However, none of the names were

Angela, just Baby Girl. You wouldn't happen to know the name of the mother, would you?"

"No. Sorry." Bowman sipped his drink and winced at the taste of the tequila.

"I'll have Red give a friend of his a call over at the Motor Vehicle Office. He might be able to give us a hand."

Bowman took another taste of his drink and sat it on the table. "Shall we head over now?"

"Might as well," Dan answered, and downed his tequila.

Chapter Fifteen

Dan and Bowman walked through the front doors of Red's Bar and Grill at a little after four. The mess had been cleaned up. A fat little man with a comb-over was unplugging the power cord to the jukebox. A tall skinny man, cell phone in hand, was leaning against a hand truck as he thumbed through the news feed of his Facebook page. He grinned every time he read something he found amusing. Clad in gray coveralls, the mismatched pair looked to Dan like a bargain basement comedy team.

"Gentlemen," Red called out from behind the bar.

"Got Laurel and Hardy fixing the old Wurlitzer, I see," Dan said. "What are we gonna do for music in the mean time?"

"I can sing if you'd like," Red offered.

"Maybe we'll just enjoy the quiet," said Dan.

Bowman climbed aboard one of the orange bars tools.

"What can I get ya?" Red asked.

"Anything but tequila," Bowman answered, then figured he'd better be more specific. "Uh, make it a rum and Coke."

Red fixed and served the drink. He fixed Dan his usual, and a whiskey and ginger ale for himself.

Dan pulled a folded-up piece of paper out of his front pocket and tossed it on the bar. "You think you could talk to your buddy, Garcia over at the county administration building and see if he can search some names for me?"

Red took the paper and unfolded it. "I don't see why not. I'm sure he doesn't have anything better to do, than a favor for you."

"He's doing the favor for you. *You're* doing the favor for me," Dan pointed out, and took a big swig of his drink.

Bowman watched as Dan guzzled the tequila. "How many drinks do you usually have in a day?" he asked.

"As many as I goddamn please. Why do you ask?"

Bowman's eyes widened. "Sorry I mentioned it."

"Yeah, but not as sorry as if you mention it twice," Dan said, and downed the rest of the drink and slid the empty glass back across the bar to Red without ever losing eye contact with Bowman. "Fill 'er up, sir."

Bowman shook his head and took a sip of his own drink.

Dan returned his attention to Red. "The three names on that list are mothers of Baby girls born in the early nineties. The babies were listed as Baby Girl, and a last name. I need to know if any of those three moms later named their daughter Angela. And also where Angela might live now."

"Sounds easy enough," Red said, and glanced up at the clock behind him. "I'll give Garcia a call in a little while."

"Tell him there's a rush on this," Dan said. "It would be nice if he could get back to you before lunch tomorrow."

"Yeah, wouldn't that be nice," Red snorted, and shoved the list in his pocket.

Bowman pulled a black leather cigar case from the side pocket of his cargo shorts. He pulled the top off to reveal four Maduro cigars, 50-ring gauge and six inches long. He turned the case over and slid a gold cigar cutter out of its pouch. "Stogie, gentlemen?" he asked, and held the case toward Dan.

"Don't mind if I do," Dan said, and grabbed one of the cigars with his thumb and index finger.

Bowman turned the case in Red's direction and he, too, took one. Bowman removed one for himself, cut the tip, and tossed the cutter on the bar in front of Dan. Red reached behind him and grabbed a small box of wooden matches off of the back bar and handed them to Bowman. All three men lit their cigars and the entire room filled with the aroma of Cuban delight.

Dan twirled the cigar in his mouth as he drew in the smoke and then slowly exhaled. "Now that's a good cigar."

"You got that right," Red said, as he pulled the stogie from his mouth and inspected the lit end.

The smoke wafted around Bowman's head. "When I get home I'll send both of you a couple of boxes."

"Thanks," Red said. "That would be awesome."

Dan smoked his cigar, sipped his drink, and had almost forgotten about Charles and Tiffany Hamilton, and Tiffany's boy toy, some kid named Clement ... *almost* forgot about them. "I spoke with Charles Hamilton this afternoon," he announced generally.

"And what did old Chuck have to say?" Red asked, and rubbed his back as though the pain had returned at the thought of them.

"He says he'll reimburse you for any pain you may have suffered."

Red took a long drag on the Maduro. "How much is my pain worth?"

"I'm hoping it's a little less than my aggravation."

"Does this have anything to do with my case?" Bowman asked.

Dan cocked his head toward Bowman. "Rich people. They think everything is about them," Dan replied. "No, Bowman, this is about me."

"He said, proving his own point," Red remarked.

"Can I finish?" Dan asked.

Red laughed. "Go ahead."

"Hamilton says those pictures will cost his wife about eight million in a divorce settlement. He says his wife has probably offered her idiot boyfriend a large chunk of change to get the pictures away from me. Hamilton will be back in town on Tuesday and until then I'm to guard them with my life."

"So what you're saying is, is that I have two days to figure up a price for my pain and suffering," Red said, blowing smoke rings into the air.

A woman sitting with her husband at one of the tables loudly cleared her throat. The three men looked over. "Excuse me," she said. "Can you gentlemen please put out those cigars? The room is filled with second-hand smoke and I can hardly breathe."

Red looked from Dan to Bowman and then back to the woman. "I'll tell you what," he said. "If you don't complain about the second-hand smoke, I won't complain about the first-hand bitching that's coming from *your* table. How's that sound, princess?"

The woman looked horrified. "Well, I never!"

"That might be your problem," Red informed her.

The woman stood and glared at her husband. "Harvey! Stand up! Let's go, now!"

Harvey stood, tucked his figurative tail between his legs, and followed his wife across the room toward the door.

"Good boy, Harvey!" Dan called out.

Red slowly shook his head. "Tourists."

Chapter Sixteen

Dan was still sitting on his bar stool at eleven thirty when Maxine walked through the door. She was dressed in blue scrubs. "Hey," she said as she walked up behind him. The dazed expression on Dan's face and the glassy look in his eyes told her everything she wanted to know.

Dan looked her up and down. "What are you, a nurse, or somthin'," he mumbled, and then laughed.

"Have you been here all day?" she asked, knowing that he probably had been.

He swayed back and forth on the stool, and his head slowly bounced around like a Dan Coast bobblehead. "Yes, Mother. Is that okay, or am I grounded?"

Maxine didn't think he was funny, this time or any other time he was in this shape.

Cindy walked down the bar toward them. "I cut him off about an hour ago. Haven't given him anything but 7Up and lime since."

Dan shook his finger at Cindy. "And I thought you

were my friend."

"I am. That's why I cut you off."

"Whatever," Dan said, and slid his glass across the bar. "One for the road, baby."

"I think you've had enough," Maxine said, and took hold of his arm.

Dan yanked his arm away. "I'll tell you when I've had enough. You don't tell me. Who are you, my wife?" He chuckled. "I'm just kidding. My wife's dead. You're the second best thing though, aren't you?"

Maxine swallowed hard. She knew she could just walk out the door and never have to deal with this shit again. She stood silently for a moment. She was hurt. She was embarrassed. And she fought back the tears she could feel welling in her eyes. She reached out and gently put her hand on his back. "Dan," she said softly. "It's time to go."

He turned and looked at her. "Okay," he said.

*****

Maxine pulled the car into Dan's driveway and shut off the engine. She looked over at her drunken boyfriend sound asleep and snoring in the passenger seat. She reached over and touched his cheek. He opened his eyes. "What's the matter?" he asked.

"We're home. Do you need help getting into the house?"

Dan straightened up in the seat. "I'm okay."

Maxine got out of the car and walked around to Dan's

side and opened his door. He took her hand and together they walked up the steps and into the house.

Buddy, lying in his bed, watched as his master stumbled into the living room.

"Should I make us a drink?" Dan asked.

"No. I'm good," Maxine responded.

Dan headed for the bar. "Maybe just a quick one."

Maxine still had his hand and pulled him toward the bedroom. "I'm tired."

"Or maybe not," Dan said, and followed her down the hall and into the bedroom. He sat on the edge of the bed and fell back. "Good night," he said.

Maxine helped him scoot further up on the mattress and removed his flip-flops. "Good night," she said.

Dan took a deep breath and exhaled. "I love you."

"I know," Maxine responded, and curled up on the bed beside him.

"Don't run in the morning, please. I don't want anything to happen to you."

"Okay. Go to sleep."

Chapter Seventeen

Dan Coast rolled over and came face to face with his dog, who had replaced Maxine on the bed. Buddy's tongue shot out of his mouth and licked Dan on the mouth. Dan pulled his head back. "Jesus Christ, dog!" he exclaimed. "Licking your ass one minute and licking *my* face the next." He wiped his mouth with the back of his hand and rolled back. He swung his feet on to the floor and noticed the note on the night stand. *Shit,* he thought. *This is it.* Had Maxine wised up? He knew he didn't deserve her, and *she* deserved a lot better than him.

Dan reached over and grabbed the note.

DAN, I RAN TO THE STORE TO GRAB MILK AND EGGS.

BE BACK IN A FEW. MAXINE

Phew, Dan exhaled, feeling like he had just dodged a bullet. He thought for sure that it was going to be the break-up note.

He pulled on his shorts and walked to the bathroom.

Dan's head felt the size of a basketball, and even felt like someone had maybe bounced it around the court for a while. He was a little nauseous and the sickly sweet smell of caramel flavored coffee wasn't helping at all. Dan poured himself a cup and walked back into the dining room. He took a sip of the coffee. He could feel the hot coffee run down his throat and hit the bottom of his stomach. "Yuck," he whispered. He glanced over at the dirty glasses and dish on the table. *I should probably do those dishes*, he thought, but instead went for the morning paper that was surly lying somewhere near the front steps. Buddy followed his friend out the door.

Dan bent to pick up the paper and his head throbbed. He straightened up and his head and stomach spun.

Edna McGee was peering out of her front window, Dan raised the paper to wave and she let the drapes drop back into position.

Buddy made his way around the side of the house along the gravel pathway that led to the backyard. Dan followed him this time. Buddy spotted his tennis ball and ran to it. Picking it up, he ran back to Dan. Dan shoved the paper into his arm pit, grabbed the ball and threw it as hard as he could toward the beach. The ball hit one of the palm trees at the edge of the yard and bounced into some morning glory vines. *There. Let's see how long it takes you to find that.*

Dan sat down in one of the Adirondack chairs, sat his cup on the ground next to him, and scanned the front page of his paper. None of the headlines caught his attention so he turned to the comics. He read them all and only laughed once at Beetle Bailey. Then he turned to the obituaries to make sure his name wasn't listed.

The back door creaked open. "How are you feeling?" Maxine called out. She felt as though she had been asking that question far too often in the last few weeks.

"Fine," Dan lied, feeling as though he had told that lie far too often in the last few weeks. *Maybe it's time to cut back for a while*, he thought.

"Hungry?"

"Maybe just some dry toast." He picked up his cup and sipped it.

"More coffee?"

"Yeah. I'll get it," Dan replied, not feeling very deserving of someone waiting on him. "I'll be right in."

Maxine said, "Okay," and let the door shut.

When Dan was finished scanning the headlines of each page without finding anything that sounded interesting, he refolded the paper, picked up his cup, and headed for the back door.

Maxine was scrambling a couple eggs for herself when Dan came in. "Toast is in the toaster," she said.

Dan walked over and manually popped up the toast. He removed a piece and bit into it with a crunch. He stared at the back of Maxine as she maneuvered the wooden spoon around the frying pan. "I'm sorry about last night," he said.

She paused for a second. "I know."

"I don't know what else to say." He took another bite of the toast.

"You don't have to say anything." Maxine reached down and turned off the burner. "You're good at saying you're sorry. It's a skill that you've practiced a lot. Maybe it's time you got to a point where you didn't have to say it as often."

Dan went from not knowing what to say, to *really* not

knowing what to say, so he kept his mouth shut and went into the dining room.

Maxine scooped her eggs onto a plate, grabbed the other piece of toast, and joined Dan at the table.

Dan glanced over at the half empty bottle of tequila on the bar and then back at his toast. The two sat quietly for a while and then Maxine asked. "Did you give the list to Red?"

"Yeah, his buddy is supposed to call sometime today with names and addresses."

"Then what?"

"I guess I give the names to Bowman and then get paid."

"That's terrible, having a sibling all these years and never knowing it." She took a bite of her eggs. "I can't imagine how he must feel."

Dan nodded in agreement. "And now, with his mother and brother dead, and his father barely hanging on, she'll soon be the only family he'll have."

"Makes me want to call *my* sister," Maxine commented.

Me too," Dan agreed. "But if I call one I'll have to call the others. My mother will hear about it and she'll call … and then I'm on the phone all day."

Maxine shook her head. "Poor you." She picked up her plate and the two glasses Dan had left from the night before. "You have company last night?" she asked, holding up the two glasses.

"Bowman stopped here to pick me up on his way to Red's last night."

Maxine took the dishes into the kitchen and placed them in the sink.

"Leave those dishes," Dan said. "I'll do them later."

"Sure ya will," Maxine called back, and turned on the water.

"Really," Dan said. "Leave them. I'll do them."

Maxine shut off the water. "You know what? I'm going to leave them. Just to prove to you that you won't do them. Let's see how long these dishes sit here in this sink." She grabbed a dish towel and dried her hands. "You should just install a dish washer."

Dan grinned. "I did install one, a few months back, but I told her *I* would do them instead."

"Funny," Maxine said.

Chapter Eighteen

Dan and Maxine were walking along Smathers Beach when Dan's cell phone rang. They both carried their flip-flops and walked barefooted in the sand, at the edge of the water.

"Yeah," Dan said into his cell.

"Coast. It's Walter Bowman."

"And?"

"And Rick Carver just called me. They think they found my brother's body."

"Where are you?" Dan asked.

"On my way to your house."

"Okay. Hang tight. I'll be there in twenty minutes."

"Is there a problem?" Maxine asked.

Dan turned and pulled her in the other direction. "We have to head back. That was Bowman. The police have found his brother's body."

"Oh my God. Where?"

"I don't know. He's on his way to my house to pick me up."

The two walked hurriedly back in the direction they had come. When they got to the corner where A1A turns into Bertha Street, Dan and Maxine proceeded carefully onto the rocks that separated the street from the private beach behind Henry's Piece of Paradise, a popular vacation rental destination. Dan held Maxine's hand as she stepped from the rocks to the beach.

"This is a private beach," an older gentleman in a lounge chair informed them as they walked by.

"No shit," Dan said. "So let's just keep this between you and me."

Maxine giggled.

The couple went on another two hundred yards and turned up the sandy path that led to Dan's backyard. Dan looked around but Bowman was nowhere in sight. Maxine followed Dan up the gravel path to the back door. The door was partially open and Dan noticed immediately that the door jamb near the striker plate was splintered. He reached into his pocket and pulled out his cell. Handing it to Maxine, he said, "Go back down by the beach. If I don't come out in five minutes call Rick."

Maxine backed down the path. "Okay. Be careful, please."

Dan waited until Maxine was halfway across the yard and then pushed the door the rest of the way open. He peeked into the kitchen. Several cupboard doors were standing open and a few drawers were pulled out. Dan glanced down at the silverware scattered about the floor. He entered the room and with every step the floorboards underneath him creaked. *Dammit*, he thought. He had never noticed the squeaking before, but now, trying to be quiet, they seemed deafening.

Dan thought about his gun under the nightstand and moved toward the hall. As he entered the hall he could see a shadow moving about through the gap below the bathroom door. He sidestepped past the door and slipped into his bedroom. The drawer was pulled from the stand, and lying on the floor. Dropping to his knees, he felt for his pistol, and grabbed the grip. His eyes shot to the closet floor. The carpeting and floor boards over his hiding place were undisturbed.

The bathroom door opened and Dan jumped to his feet, pressing his back up against the wall, to the right of the doorway. With his gun to his chest and pointing upward he could feel the beating of his heart against the cold steel of the barrel. He waited silently as the intruder exited the bathroom and walked down the hall toward him.

Dan watched the door and the second he saw the man's nose enter the room, he swung. The side of the pistol connected with the man's face and his head snapped back.

"Jesus Christ!" Bowman shouted.

Dan jumped into the doorway with his weapon trained on Bowman's forehead. When he realized who it was he shouted, "Bowman! What the Christ are you doing here?"

Bowman, with his hand over his mouth, responded, "I thold you I wath coming here." He pulled his hand away from his face, revealing his cut lip and chipped front tooth.

"Ouch," Dan said. "Are you by yourself?"

Bowman nodded. "Yeth. Who would I be with?"

Dan shrugged. "I don't know. Who did this to my house?" he asked, looking around the room at the mess.

"I have no idea. It wath like thith when I got here."

Dan grinned. "You thound really funny," he said, mocking Bowman.

Bowman didn't see the humor. He turned and walked back down the hall and returned to the bathroom.

When Dan walked by he glanced in at Bowman inspecting his mouth in the mirror. "What the hell were you doing in the bathroom when I got here, anyway?" he asked.

"Taking a pith. What do you think?"

Dan laughed again. "Taking a pith." He lifted the back of his shirt and slid the barrel of the 9mm into his waistband at the small of his back, and let the shirt drop over it. "Stop being such a baby. It's a tiny little chip. I'll drop you by the dentist tomorrow."

Bowman ran his index finger across the chip. "I thwallowed it."

"It's not gonna kill ya," Dan responded, and then went to the back door and hollered through the screen. "Come on in, Maxine! Everything is fine!"

Maxine had been waiting on the sandy path that led to the beach. She jogged up to the house when Dan yelled. "Wow! What a mess," she said as she entered the kitchen. "Is anything missing?"

"No. They didn't find what they were looking for," Dan responded.

Bowman walked into the kitchen. "Hi, Maxthine."

Chapter Nineteen

Maxine had wanted to stay at Dan's and clean up the mess but Dan told her he didn't want her to be there alone, so he sent her home to her own place. He felt she would be much safer there.

Bowman took a right on to A1A, toward Stock Island. "Where is this place where they found my brother?" he asked. He had learned quickly to compensate for the chipped tooth and was speaking much clearer.

"Right up here on the left," Dan responded. "About a mile and a half."

Bowman watched the street signs. "So, how come you don't have a car?"

"Wrecked it," Dan responded.

"What *did* you drive?"

"Porsche, 911 convertible—2006 model."

"Nice. I have an '09. Going to get another one?"

"I don't know." Dan pointed. "It's right here."

A Key West patrol car was parked in the median with its light bar flashing. One of the southbound lanes had been blocked with orange cones and an officer directed traffic around them. Bowman pulled to the left side shoulder and parked.

The two got out of the car and the officer stopped traffic as they crossed the road. Dan recognized the police officer as the same one he had threatened with a broken tequila bottle last Christmas morning. Dan nodded to the officer, who in turn, silently mouthed the words *fuck you*.

"Friend of yours?" Bowman asked.

"Acquaintance," Dan replied.

Dan and Bowman walked down an access road past a sign that read, For Sale: Enchanted Island, Private Offshore Islands. About fifty feet down the road they came to another patrol car sitting near a metal gate made from two-inch steel pipe. The gate was open and they continued on down the road. They passed another officer on foot who gave Dan a friendly nod.

"He must not know you," Bowman said.

"Obviously," Dan responded. "Must be new."

"Maybe you had better befriend him before the other officers corrupt him."

"Maybe," Dan agreed.

They could see the coroner's van near the end of the road as well as two other cruisers and an ambulance. Chief Rick Carver met them at the front of the coroner's van. The uniform of the day was a shirt two sizes too small stretched around his massive belly and pit stains the size of the Gulf of Mexico. Gold-rimmed aviator sunglasses, the chief's trademark, topped the ensemble. Whether or not they lent him the air of authority and mystery he intended was in the eye of the beholder. Dan was firmly in the "not" camp.

"What the hell happened to you?" He asked Bowman, noticing the chipped tooth, and slightly swollen lip.

"It's a long story," Bowman replied.

"Did he hit you?" Rick asked. "Just let me know if you want to press charges."

"I didn't hit him," Dan protested.

An EMT wheeled a gurney toward the rear of the coroner's van. Rick turned and motioned for Dan and Bowman to follow.

"Fisherman found the deceased in the water … about twenty yards out from shore," Rick informed them. "Coroner says it looks like he's been there a couple days. Probably since right after you found him on the beach. It's a wonder the gators hadn't got him yet."

"Real delicate choice of words there, Rick," said Dan

Rick shot an apologetic glance at Bowman, whose face was lit green. "Sorry. Think you can handle ID'ing the body?"

"Yes," said Bowman in a strangled voice.

Rick nodded to the EMT who began unzipping the olive green body bag. Bowman swayed and Dan grabbed his arm.

"That's him," Dan and Bowman said in unison.

Rick nodded again and the EMT zipped up the bag. Together he and the coroner lifted the gurney into the back of the van and slammed the door.

"I ran a check on your brother after you came to the police station the other day," Rick commented. "Looks like he's been in and out of trouble most of his life."

Dan glanced over at Bowman and then back at Rick.

Bowman nodded. "Yeah, Warren … had a rough life."

Rick pulled a small black note pad from his back pocket and flipped it open. "Thirty days in King County Detention Center for forged checks when he was nineteen. Six months in Columbia County for petit larceny at the age of twenty-three. He spent his twenty-fifth birthday doing ninety days in Clark County for aggravated assault. And then back to King County for one year following an involuntary manslaughter conviction, for which he is still on parole. Sounds more like the people around him have had a rough life."

"Whoa, Rick," Dan said. "go a little easy. He just lost his brother."

Bowman stood in stony silence.

"I also ran a check on you, Bowman," Rick informed him. "Seems you've never been in any trouble at all. I guess that makes you the good son."

"I guess," Bowman agreed.

The three men watched as the van started and pulled away.

"You know, Coast, there was a part of me that hoped you were wrong," Bowman said. "That maybe Warren wasn't dead. Maybe he just got up and walked away from the beach. Maybe he was somewhere hurt or something."

Dan put his hand on Bowman's back. "Sorry, pal."

Bowman turned to Rick. "Where are they taking his body?"

Rick pushed his sunglasses up his sweaty nose with his middle finger. "They'll take him to the morgue. There will be an autopsy due to the circumstances surrounding his death and there'll be an investigation."

"How long before I'll be able to have his body sent home?"

"No more than a couple days," Rick answered. He shook Bowman's hand and said, "I'll be in touch."

"Thanks, Chief," Bowman said.

Dan and Bowman walked back down the road to the car. Bowman didn't say much, he just stared at the blacktop as they walked along. When they got to the car he tossed Dan the keys. "Would you mind driving?" he asked.

Dan snatched the keys out of the air. "I don't have my—sure, I guess."

Dan whipped the Lincoln into the southbound lane and headed for home.

Bowman looked at his watch. "I wonder what time Red will call. I'm starting to get a little anxious."

Dan glanced down at the clock on the dashboard. "I thought we would have heard from him by now."

"Should we run by the bar?" Bowman asked.

"Might as well. I'm starting to get hungry."

*****

Dan walked into the bar first. "Hear anything from Garcia, over at the DMV?" he asked.

"You'll be the first to know," Red responded. "Well, third to know, I guess."

Dan climbed aboard his usual bar stool and Bowman sat down beside him.

110

"Can I get you guys something to drink?" Red asked.

"A Coke," Bowman said.

Dan caught himself drumming his fingers nervously on the bar top, something he couldn't ever remember doing. Just saying the words was going to be tough, much less, actually going through with it. He rehearsed the words mentally and spat them out in a wad.

"I'll just have a 7Up."

Red tried not to look surprised. "Coming right up." He poured Dan's soda. "You want a lime with that?"

"What's that supposed to mean?" Dan asked.

"Nothing," Red answered. "You usually have a lime in your drink."

"Well I'm not having a drink, am I? I'm having a goddamn soda. So just give me the soda and stop worrying about what I want in it."

"Oh-*kay,*" Red answered and slid the drink across the bar. "Here ya go, touchy."

"No lime for me, either," Bowman remarked.

"Don't worry. I was afraid to ask—don't want to get my head bit off … again."

"Keep talking," Dan said.

Red's cell phone began vibrating across the bar. He picked it up and answered. "Hello?"

"Hey, Red, it's Garcia. Got that information you needed."

Red turned, grabbed a pen and a napkin off the back bar. "Shoot," he said, and began jotting down an address and a phone number. When he finished he said thanks and hung up.

"Well, do we have a winner?" Dan asked.

"Did he find her?" Bowman asked excitedly.

Red turned back and laid the napkin in front of Bowman. "Garcia said he did a search of each birth mother and the name Elizabeth Breck turned up one relative in the area. A young woman by the name of Angela."

"Bingo!" Dan said.

Bowman stared at Red's chicken scratch. ANGELA BRECK, 3708 PEARLMAN COURT. Below the address was a phone number. He slid the napkin over in front of Dan. "Will you call for me?"

Dan pulled out his cell and held the napkin at arm's length to see it more clearly.

"Forgot your glasses?" Bowman asked.

"I don't wear glasses," Dan snapped.

He dialed the number and a woman's voice said, "This is Angela. You know what to do."

"This message is for Angela Breck. My name is Dan Coast. I live here in Key West and I'm working with a gentleman who has been trying to locate you." Dan paused for a second wondering exactly how much information he should give her. "Um … he thinks he may be your brother. Please give me a call back at this number when you get this message. Thanks." Dan hit the end call icon and placed his cell on the bar.

"What's next?" Bowman asked.

"I have some lunch and then go home and clean my house."

Chapter Twenty

It was a little after three when Walter Bowman pulled up in front of Dan's house and let him out.

"So, you'll call me when she gets back to you?" Bowman asked.

"You'll be the first to know," Dan answered.

Bowman managed a grin. "The third."

"Oh, yeah."

Dan shut the car door and walked up the path to his front steps carrying a plastic bag containing his left-overs from lunch. Buddy met him at the door as if someone had phoned ahead telling him about the coming treat. His tail wagged and his front paws bounced off the hard wood floor. His whine sounded more like pain than excitement. He sniffed at the bag.

"Hold on, dog," Dan said. "Let me get in the damn door."

Buddy's food dish sat on the floor next to his bed.

Dan dumped the contents of the doggy bag into the bowl. The steak bone clinked against the side of the dish and Buddy scooped it up immediately and began crunching.

Dan looked about the place assessing the mess. Both doors on the bar were open, as well as the two drawers. One of the drawers was on the floor with its contents scattered about. He glanced over at his lamp lying broken on the floor. *Where to start*, he thought. *Where to start.*

*****

Dan was in the kitchen sweeping the last bits of a shattered glass into a dust pan when Bev knocked on the back door. "Have a little accident?" she asked.

"You might say that," Dan answered.

Buddy jumped up from his bed and ran to the back door to greet his friend.

Bev pulled open the screen door and went in. "How ya doin, pal?" she asked as she scratched the dog behind the ears. "Haven't seen much of you guys lately."

Dan walked over and dumped the broken glass into the garbage can. "Yeah, been pretty busy the last few days."

"I figured."

"How's fantasy camp going?" Dan asked, shoving the broom and dustpan back between the cupboard and the refrigerator.

"Funny," Bev answered. "It's going fine. It's a lot of fun going down there and working out."

"I bet it is. Maybe I better get down there and pump

me some iron."

Bev ignored Dan's ribbing. "Are we going to have a drink, or what?"

Dan glanced over at the clock on the microwave. *Made it till 4:13*, he thought. *Sure, why not*. He turned and went into the dining room to grab a couple glasses off the bar. On his way back into the kitchen he heard a car engine rev.

Buddy's ears perked up and he let out low quiet growl.

Dan handed the glasses to Bev, turned, and went back into the dining room. The engine roared again, this time louder and longer. He could see the black Mustang through the window in the front door. As he walked to the door Buddy followed.

Dan opened the door and Buddy ran past him toward the car. Dan tried to grab his collar but missed, "Buddy!" he yelled. The dog barked as he ran toward the car. At the edge of the sidewalk Buddy stopped.

Dan picked up his pace and just as he got to the car the driver floored it, spinning the tires, and kicking up dust. At the end of the street he turned the corner and disappeared.

Dan reached down and patted Buddy's side. "We'll get that bastard next time, pal."

Dan turned and went back inside. Buddy walked down the sidewalk toward Bev's house.

Bev had made both drinks and handed one to Dan.

"Sit outside?" Bev suggested.

"Sure," Dan said, and went to the cupboard for the bag of Cool Ranch Doritos, he knew were waiting for him.

As he pulled the bag of chips from the cabinet he

heard the tires squeal as they slid around the corner. Dan froze as he heard the roar of the engine.

Buddy barked twice, and then came a thud.

Dan felt Buddy's pain-filled yelps in his chest and gut. Every hair on his body stood on end.

Dan was running for the front door. It felt like a nightmare, as his feet and legs didn't seem to move fast enough.

Buddy's calls for help had stopped by the time Dan hit the screen door, ripping it from its hinges. He leapt from the porch, over the steps, to the ground. He saw Buddy lying at the edge of the street in front of Bev's house.

Dan ran as fast as he could, dropping to his knees when he reached his best friend.

Buddy tried to pick up his head to look Dan in the eye. "Don't move, pal," Dan said.

There was blood on Buddy's mouth and around his nose.

"Is he okay?" Bev called out, as she hurried down the sidewalk toward them.

"Get your keys!" Dan cried out.

Bev ran for her front door.

Dan looked up and saw Edna McGee on her front porch. One hand was on her chest, the other covered her mouth.

"Goddammit!" Dan said. "You're gonna be okay. You're gonna be okay." Dan stroked Buddy's side. He could feel Buddy's chest expand with every breath. He inspected the dog for injuries as he waited.

Bev came out the door and pointed her key fob at the

mini-van. The side door slid open.

Dan scooped up his dog in his arms and walked as quickly and carefully as he could toward the van. He laid Buddy on the floor and climbed in. Bev shut the door behind him.

Chapter Twenty-One

Bev took her foot off the gas as she approached the red light at the intersection of Flagler Avenue and Kennedy Drive. She yanked the wheel to the left, hopping the concrete median and the van bounced into the parking lot of the Lower Keys Animal Clinic. She slammed on the brakes and Dan rocked forward against the back of the passenger seat.

Buddy's eyes registered fear and confusion. "You're gonna be okay," Dan whispered for the hundredth time.

The door slid open and Dan carried Buddy into the clinic. "Please!" he shouted. "Somebody help me. He was hit by a car."

Bev entered and let the door swing shut behind them.

The receptionist behind the counter jumped to her feet and ran around the desk to a door. "Right in here," she said. She held the door as Dan walked through. "Right there on the table," she instructed.

Dan did as he was told.

"Dr. Lee!" the receptionist hollered.

Within seconds the veterinarian rounded the corner. "What happened?" he asked.

"A car hit him," Dan answered. "Please, help him. He's the only thing I have that's—you gotta help him."

Dan stepped back as Dr. Lee moved around the table. He stroked Buddy's head with genuine caring. "Didja get the license plate number, fella?" he jested, probing the dog's body with expert gentleness

Dan's eyes went to Buddy's chest as he backed up against the wall. The breathing was more ragged now. He reached into his pocket, pulled out his cell phone, and dialed. "Red. Meet me at my house in twenty minutes."

"What are you going to do?" Bev asked.

Dan ignored the question. "Stay with him, Bev," he said, and then grabbed the doctor's arm and locked eyes with him. "Don't let him die."

"I'll do everything I can," Dr. Lee answered.

Bev tossed Dan her car keys.

Dan reached down and touched Buddy's nose. "I'll see you in a little bit." He spun and ran out the door.

Chapter Twenty-Two

Dan drove straight home and went right for the pistol under the nightstand. When he exited the house through the front he had to jump over the screen door that lay busted at the bottom of the steps.

Red screeched to a halt in front of the house. "What's going on!" he yelled through the passenger side window.

Dan ran to the car and jumped in. "Go!" he shouted.

Red floored it. "Where?" he asked.

"Key Largo."

"Black Mustang?"

"Black Mustang."

The tires squealed as Red rounded the corner on to George Street. "Are you gonna tell me what happened?" he asked.

Dan was rubbing his temples with his fingertips. "He hit my dog."

Red shook his head. "God dammit. Is he gonna be okay?"

"I don't know. He's at the vet's now. Bev is there with him."

"We'll get the son of a bitch."

Dan put his head back against the headrest.

Red leaned forward and turned on the radio. James Taylor was singing "Fire and Rain."

Dan turned his head and stared out the window as he thought back to the day he and Alex first saw the cardboard sign on Elm Street in Cooperstown. With a Sharpie marker the homeowner had written FOR SALE: BORDER COLLIE/LAB MIX.

"Oh my God, look how cute he is," Alex gushed.

"Yeah, he's cute alright," was Dan's reply. "Cuter than a yard full of dog shit."

"Come on, let's get him … please," she begged.

"All right, but you're carrying the baggie and picking up the crap when we walk him. Remember, you want a dog, not me. It's your dog, not mine."

At that moment, Buddy staring death in the face, Dan decided the mutt had been as much his as Alex's all along.

*****

It was after nine by the time Red veered left across the intersection onto Ocean Bay Drive, in Key Largo. "How do you want to do this?" Red asked.

"Park in the same place we parked last time," Dan

replied.

"Will do."

Red took the first left he came to and then another quick left onto Point Pleasant Drive. He drove about halfway down the block, pulled to the side of the street, and shut off the engine.

"I think we should have parked in one of the parking lots out on US1," he said. "If anyone follows us out of there, we'll be stuck at this end of the street, and have to drive back through them."

Dan pulled the 9mm from the back of his waistband and ejected the magazine. He pulled back the slide and inspected the chamber. Jamming the magazine back into the grip, he released the slide.

"No one's following us out of there," he said.

The two men climbed from Red's vehicle and Dan returned the pistol to his waistband. His cell phone rang. He pulled it from his pocket, and looked at the screen. "Shit," he said. "It's Bowman's sister."

Red slammed his door. "Are ya gonna answer it?"

Dan tossed the phone through the open window onto the passenger seat. "I'll call her back."

Red started up the street toward the Hamilton house and Dan followed close behind.

"Do you have a plan?" Red asked.

"Do I ever?" Dan replied.

Before they even reached the block fence they could hear the sounds of laughter and splashing water. When they got there Red peeked over the fence. The yard lights were on this time and Red saw Clement lying on a blow up mattress in the center of the pool. He had a half empty bottle of Mic Ultra wedged between his legs, and his arms were folded behind his head.

Tiffany Hamilton lay in a lounge chair between the house and the pool. Two other men about the same age as Clement swam around the pool, and a second woman in her late forties sat on the edge dangling her feet in the water.

"Like I said," Red asked. "How do you want to do this?" He turned to hear Dan's reply but Dan was gone. Red glanced back over the fence to see Dan bursting through the gate. "Shit!"

Red spun and ran around the fence to the gate. By the time he reached Dan's side, Dan had his weapon drawn and trained on Clement.

"Get out of the pool, asshole" Dan said calmly.

"Kiss my ass," Clement replied. One of his friends chuckled.

Dan fired the 9mm hitting the mattress between Clements legs. The raft began deflating and Clement rolled off and swam to the side.

Dan pointed the weapon at the kid who laughed. "The next person who snickers gets one in the forehead. Understand?"

The douche slowly nodded yes and inched toward the edge of the pool.

Red walked around the pool as he kept an eye on the swimmers.

Dan aimed the gun back at Clement. "You get out of the pool. You other two stay in the pool."

One of the other two was already pulling himself out of the water. Red placed the toe of his shoe on the young man's forehead and shoved him back in. "He said stay in the pool, stupid," Red instructed.

Tiffany reached for her cell phone that lay on the wicker end table next to her. "Don't," Dan said, and she yanked her hand back.

Red walked over, grabbed the cell, and pitched it into the water.

Dan looked over at the other cougar. She hadn't moved. "Let me guess," Dan said. "Your husband is also out of town on business."

The woman shook her head yes. "Portland."

"Which one of these scumbags is your toy?" Dan asked.

"Those two," she said, pointing.

"Did someone say hog roast?" Red asked.

One of the young men grinned.

"No grinning either," Red informed him.

Clement slowly walked up the steps out of the pool. Dan made his way toward him. Clement was too cocky or too ignorant to be scared so when Dan reached him he brought the pistol's grip down on his nose. The nose shattered and blood exploded from Clement's nostrils. Suddenly he knew how to be scared. He dropped to his knees and covered his mouth and nose with both hands.

"That's for my dog," Dan said. Then he smashed the barrel of the 9mm against the side of Clements head. "And that's for following my girlfriend."

"Stop!" Tiffany screamed. "Don't hurt him."

Red shot her a look. "I think it's too late for that."

The two men in the pool were still cringing. They too had learned to worry a little.

Dan brought up his foot and kicked Clement in the chest, knocking him on his back. He lay on the concrete, looking up at his abuser.

"That's for ransacking my house," Dan informed him.

Clement waved Dan off. "Stop … please … no more."

Dan switched hands with his gun, then reached down and grabbed Clement by the front of his swim trunks. Dan picked the kid up by his trunks and dragged him to the shed that sat in the corner of the yard. At the shed Dan dropped him and opened the door. Inside the shed was the pump, containers of chemicals, a few pool toys, and a leaf net.

"Get in," Dan instructed.

Clement crab walked backwards into the shed.

Dan placed the barrel of his weapon against Clement's package and applied pressure. Clement winced.

"You come out of that shed and I'm still here, I'll shoot your dick off." Dan nodded toward Tiffany Hamilton. "You ever go near her or any other married woman for the rest of your life, and I'll shoot your dick off. You ever come near me, my home, or anyone I've ever met, and what will I do?" Dan asked, cocking his head toward Clement and placing his hand behind his ear.

"You'll shoot my dick off," Clement answered.

"Quick learner," Dan said and closed the shed door.

Dan returned the 9mm to his right hand and started walking toward Tiffany Hamilton. "Please don't hurt me," she pleaded.

"Oh, I'm not going to *hurt* you," Dan replied. "I'm going to *help* you, or at least give you the opportunity to help yourself."

Tiffany looked confused. "I don't understand."

Dan pulled his camera's memory card from his pocket. "This memory card contains the pictures your husband hired me to take of you and your little friend over there in the shed."

"And?" Tiffany asked.

"*And* how much are they worth to you?"

"I don't know, exactly."

"Just round it down to the amount you have in the house."

"We don't keep money in the house."

Dan shoved the card back in his pocket. "Have it your way," he said and turned toward the gate.

"Wait!" Tiffany shouted. "We have five thousand in the safe."

Dan pointed higher.

"Ten thousand."

Dan pointed upward again.

"Okay! Fifteen."

"That sounds better. Red, go in with her and make sure she doesn't do anything stupid."

Red followed Tiffany into the house.

Dan looked around at the other three. "Nice night for a swim," he said. "I should have brought my suit."

"You don't need a suit," the cougar said, and gave Dan a wink.

"Really?" Dan chuckled. "Aren't I a little old for you?"

"You're only as old as you feel," she said.

"Well, most days I feel sixty."

Red and Tiffany returned to the pool. Tiffany was carrying three stacks of hundred dollar bills. She handed them to Dan.

"Pleasure doing business with you," Dan said, as he took the money.

Tiffany just sneered at him.

Dan and Red turned and walked back through the gate.

As they neared the car Red's cell phone vibrated in his back pocket. "Hello?" he answered. There was a pause and then he said, "He left his phone in the car. Here he is." Red handed his phone to Dan.

"Yeah," Dan said. "Oh … hey, Bev." Dan's stomach tightened as he listened. "Good. We'll be back in a couple hours." Dan hung up the phone and handed it back to his friend.

"Everything okay?" Red asked.

"He's gonna be fine. Two broken ribs and his lung was punctured. They're going to keep him for a couple days." Dan let out a long sigh. "Goddamn dog."

The two men climbed into the car. Red started the engine and pulled away from the curb.

"See, no one is following us," Dan pointed out.

Red grinned as he pulled onto US1. "Did you see the look on her face when she handed you that cash?"

"That was pretty funny, all right," Dan agreed. "But I would love to see the look on her face tomorrow night when she finds out I made copies of the photographs and sold *them* to her husband."

"Wow!" Red said. "You really are an asshole."

"Never said I wasn't."

Chapter Twenty-Three

"Would you believe I haven't had a drink all day?" Dan asked. He retrieved his cell phone from his pocket and laid it on the bar next to him. He thought about returning Angela Breck's call. He glanced up at the clock over the back bar and changed his mind.

Red was making two margaritas for a young couple at the end of the bar who couldn't keep their hands off of each other. "Would you believe I don't give a shit one way or the other?" he responded.

"I believe that," Dan said.

Red delivered the drinks to the two love birds and returned. "Tequila, Seven, and lime?" he asked.

"You know it," Dan replied.

Red made the drink and slid it across the bar to his friend. "There ya go, pal. Now you can't say you haven't had a drink all day."

"It was fun while it lasted."

"Was it?"

"Not really." Dan downed the drink in two gulps. "Another, sir."

Red did as he was asked and Dan sipped the second drink much slower.

"Maxine meeting you here?" Red asked.

"Of course. It's either that, or I walk home." Dan replied.

"It's not like you haven't walked home before."

"Never sober."

"When are you getting a new car?"

"As soon as I get my license back."

"You don't need a driver's license to buy a car."

"I know," Dan said. "But I'm stupid, and if I buy a car I'll start driving it, get caught without a license, and then lose it for even longer."

Red shook his head in agreement as he stood polishing the bar glasses. "You are stupid, my friend."

"Thank you."

"No problem."

Dan sipped his drink and then looked up at the clock again. "Maybe I will walk home," he said. "I have a long day ahead of me tomorrow and Maxine isn't getting out of work tonight until midnight."

"You want to take the Volkswagen Bug?" Red asked. "It's parked around back by the dumpster.

"Good place for it. You want me driving that thing without a license?"

"If ya get caught I'll just say you stole it."

Dan downed his drink and said, "I'll pass." He slid off his bar stool, turned, made his way across the bar room, and disappeared through the front door.

*****

As Dan walked up the sidewalk toward his house Bev drove by in her mini-van and pulled into her driveway. Dan paused when he got to his house and waited for Bev to get out. When she finally did, he called over, "Where the Christ are you coming from at this hour?"

Bev smiled. "If you must know, I had a date."

"I knew that pumping iron was going to lead to nothing but trouble," Dan said.

"Hey," Bev said, putting up her arms and twirling her sexy-and-svelt-early-sixty-body in a circle. "When ya got it, ya got it."

"Where did you meet this guy?"

"At the gym."

Dan rolled his eyes. "At the gym," he repeated. "Let's make us a couple drinks and you can fill me in on this muscle head."

Bev giggled. "Okay. I gotta run in the house for a second. You make the drinks and I'll be right over."

"Sounds good," Dan said. "But if ya giggle one more time like that, the night is over."

"I'll try not to," Bev hollered over her shoulder, as she trotted down the sidewalk.

Dan picked up his broken screen door, leaned it

against the front of the house, and went inside. As he crossed the living room he looked down at Buddy's empty bed, and then at the photograph of Alex on the table next to it. He wondered what time the vet opened in the morning. He missed his dog and wanted to be there first thing in the morning. *Guess Maxine is right*, he mused. *I am a softie masquerading as a tough guy.*

Dan and Bev exited their back doors at the same time. Dan carried the two drinks and handed Bev hers as they met at the two Adirondack chairs near the fire pit.

Bev sat down, let out a sigh, and then sipped her tequila. "First, let's talk about where you went."

"I went to Key Largo to kick the shit out of a douche bag and swindle an old whore out of fifteen thousand dollars."

"Sounds like a productive day."

"I guess," Dan agreed. "Now let's hear about the gym rat you're dating."

"We're not dating. We went on one date."

"And why didn't I hear about this earlier?"

"Because I didn't want to hear *this*."

"So how old is this kid?"

Bev laughed. "He's not a kid. He's seventy-one years old."

Dan did a spit take. "Seventy-one years old? What the Christ do you want with an old man like that?"

"A second ago you were about to give me hell because you thought it was someone too young, now you're giving me hell because he's too old. What age of man do you think I should be dating?"

"Someone your own age," Dan replied. "Sixty, or

sixty-one."

Bev had never told Dan her exact age; his guess was alarmingly close to the mark. "Whatever," she said, and took another sip of her drink.

"What's he do?" Dan asked.

"He's retired."

"From what?"

"NASA."

"Yeah, right. That's not even a good lie. NASA. And I bet he moonlighted with the CIA."

"If he did, he didn't mention it."

"What kind of car does he drive?"

"It's a little red convertible … an MG, I think he said."

"MG Midget."

"Yeah that's it."

"So what's this phony's name?"

"Larson."

Dan started to take a drink and froze. "Kip Larson?"

"Yes. How did you know?"

"Kip Larson is an astronaut."

"I know. I just said that."

Maxine's car pulled into the driveway. Her headlights lit up the backyard for a second and Bev glanced out toward the street.

Dan pulled out his phone and typed Kip Larson, astronaut into the search bar. When a picture popped up he turned the phone toward Bev. "This guy?"

"Yeah, that's Kip."

Dan downed the rest of his drink. "This. Is. *Awesome*! When do I get to meet him?"

"I don't know if I'm even going out with him again."

"The hell you're not! He's Kip Larson, for Chrissakes."

"He's a nice guy, but he brags about himself an awful lot."

Dan shook his head in disbelief. "Yeah! Because he's Kip Larson!"

"He asked me out to dinner this Friday," Bev said, "but I haven't accepted, yet."

The back door swung open and Maxine walked down the steps. She had made herself a rum and Coke. "Room for one more?" she called out.

Dan jumped up to get Maxine a chair. "We're going out to dinner Friday night with Bev and Kip Larson," he said, excitedly.

Maxine asked, "Who is Kip Larson?"

Dan rolled his eyes. "Who's Kip Larson? What's wrong with you people?"

"*We* were never twelve-year-old boys," Bev joked.

"I have to work Friday," Maxine said.

"That's what sick days are for," Dan observed. "Kip Larson invites us to dinner … we go to dinner."

"Kip didn't invite you to dinner," Bev reminded him.

"Whatever," said Dan.

"I'm sure I can get the night off," Maxine said. "I'll just tell them it's Kip Larson."

Dan clapped his hands together. "Exactly! It's a date."

Bev sipped her drink. "Great. I'll let Kip know."

Dan gazed out over the beach with a stupid grin on his face. "This is awesome. Dinner with Kip Larson."

Chapter Twenty-Four

Dan and Maxine were waiting in the parking lot of The Lower Keys Animal Clinic when the first employee arrived. Dan swung open the door and jumped from the car.

"Good morning Mr. Coast," the receptionist said with a smile.

"Good morning," Dan returned.

"We don't open till nine."

Dan pointed at the keys in the woman's hand. "Looks like you're opening now," he said. "I was hoping I could see Buddy."

"Of course, Mr. Coast."

"Thanks. And call me Dan."

"I will, and you can call me Roberta."

Maxine joined Dan at the door. Roberta unlocked it and led them through the waiting room into the back where Buddy lay on a mattress with a white blanket over him. He turned his head and looked at Dan but didn't move.

A vet tech walked into the room and said, "We're keeping him sedated for most of today. He'll be in and out but he won't feel like moving around. We want to give those ribs a rest."

"Thanks," Dan said, and knelt down beside his dog and put his hand on Buddy's head. "How ya feelin', boy?"

Buddy turned his head and licked Dan's hand.

Maxine wiped a tear from the corner of her eye.

"We'll have you out of here in no time," Dan told Buddy. "We'll get a couple steaks and then play ball on the beach."

Buddy licked the back of Dan's hand one more time and then closed his eyes.

"He'll sleep a lot today," the tech said. "He's going to be fine, Mr. Coast."

Dan reached up and shook the tech's hand. "Thanks for everything," he said, and then leaned down and kissed Buddy on the side of the head. "I'll stop back later, pal."

As they walked across the parking lot back to the car Maxine put her hand on Dan's back and rubbed.

"Damn dog," Dan said.

When they got in the car Dan pulled his cell phone from his pocket.

"Where to?" Maxine asked.

Dan hit the voice mail icon on his phone. "Somewhere with eggs and sausage." He put the phone to his ear.

Maxine started the car, put it in gear, and drove out of the parking lot onto Kennedy Drive.

Mr. Coast, this is Angela Breck. I got your message last night. I ... um, I don't really know what to say. I never knew my father, and my mother never talked about him. If at all possible, could you call me back before nine tomorrow morning?

Dan glanced at the clock on the dashboard. 8:40. He hit the call back button.

"Hello?" Angela said.

"Angela, this is Dan Coast."

"Mr. Coast, I was hoping you would call back. I assume the man who's searching for me and believes he's my brother, wishes to meet me."

"That's correct," Dan said.

"I would feel most comfortable if we met in public."

"Of course."

"I take my lunch at noon. Can he meet me then ... in Bayview Park?"

"I'll make sure of it. I'll give him a call and he'll see you there."

"Thank you, Mr. Coast. Good bye."

Dan said, "Good bye" and hung up.

"She wants to meet?" Maxine asked.

"Yup. At noon. I better give Bowman a call and let him know."

Maxine took a right off of Flagler Avenue onto White Street.

"Bowman?" Dan said into his phone.

"Yeah, Dan, what's up?"

"Got a hold of Angela this morning. She wants to

meet you in Bayview Park at noon. I promised her you would be there."

"Um, yeah, okay. Dan, can you come with me?"

"Come with you?"

"Yes. I don't know if this is something I can do alone." Bowman explained. "I would feel more comfortable if there was a third party present for the meeting."

"I guess I can."

"Thanks, Dan. Thanks for everything. I'll pick you up at your house at eleven thirty."

"I'll see you then," Dan replied, and hung up the cell.

Maxine turned left at Eaton Street. "Everything good?" she asked.

"He wants me to be there for the meeting."

"I figured he would. With his brother gone, he probably doesn't want to go through this alone."

"I guess."

Maxine parked across the street from Pepe's Café and Steakhouse, renowned as the eldest eatery in the Keys. "Here we are."

Dan looked across the street at the restaurant's Plain Jane facade. "Huh. Never been here before."

"Yeah, I figured."

"The sign says 'a fairly good place to eat for a long time.' That's not much of a recommendation."

"Oh, Dan, you're such a picky bastard. This place has been here forever, and Key West Magazine says it's the best place for breakfast. Come on, broaden your horizons."

Dan sighed. "Do they have eggs and sausage?"

"All you can eat."

"We'll see about that."

Chapter Twenty-Five

It was exactly eleven-thirty when Dan, splitting at the seams from the best breakfast he'd ever had (not that he'd admit it to Maxine), heard Walter Bowman hit the horn. He peered out his front window at the big black Lincoln Town Car.

"He's here. I'm leaving," Dan called out to Maxine.

"Okay. See you in a bit," she hollered back from the kitchen. "Good luck."

"Um … thanks," Dan said, on his way out the door. He climbed into Bowman's car and away they went.

"So, where is this Bayview Park?" Bowman asked.

"Just turn right, here on George Street and then go all the way to Catherine Street."

Bowman took the left onto George as Dan instructed. "How did she sound?" he asked. "Did she sound excited, or nervous?"

"I dunno," Dan answered. "Neither, really."

"Huh. Did she tell you anything about herself? Is she married? Does she have children?"

"All I know is that she works at the middle school."

"Teacher?"

Dan shot Bowman an annoyed look. "She could be the freakin' janitor, for all I know. Why don't you wait and ask *her* all these questions, for Chrissakes?"

"Yeah, I guess you're right."

There was silence for a few minutes and then Dan asked, "You know who Kip Larson is?"

"Never heard of him," Bowman responded. "Why do you ask?"

Dan shrugged his shoulders in disappointment. "Never mind."

"*Should* I know him?"

"He was an astronaut."

"Like, a walked on the moon astronaut?"

"Well, no, he never walked on the moon."

"I've always thought all that moon landing stuff was a hoax."

Dan rolled his eyes. "Left here," he announced as they came to Catherine Street. "The school is up here on the right—go past it and take a right on Pearl Street."

Bowman studied the middle school building as they drove by. "Did you go to school here?" he asked.

"No," Dan replied. "I'm not from here."

Bowman turned right at Pearl Street. "Oh, where are you from?"

"Upstate New York." Dan pointed toward some

empty parking spaces. "Right here, then a quick left."

Bowman maneuvered the big Lincoln into a spot between a red Ford Focus and a turd-brown Plymouth Duster. Directly in front of them, across a pond, and through some trees was the Key West Police Station. Behind them was Bayview Park.

"How will we know it's her?" Bowman asked.

"She said she would be wearing a pink carnation."

"Really?"

"No."

Bowman shook his head and muttered, "Asshole."

"I heard that."

Dan swung open the car door and it hit the Duster with a thud. He looked down. The Duster was about four inches over the parking stripe. "What the Christ? What's so hard about parking between two straight lines?" He squeezed out between the two vehicles.

Bowman asked, "You bitch a lot about little stuff, don't you?"

"Bitch is my middle name."

The two men walked across Jose Marti Drive. When they got to the grass they stopped and scanned the area. Sitting on a bench under a palm tree was a young woman about the right age. She was texting on her cell phone. They both stared at her.

"Should I holler something?" Bowman asked.

"Sure," Dan said.

"*What*?"

"Hey?"

Bowman raised his arm over his head and waved.

"Hey!" he shouted.

The young woman looked up. So did the other four people in the park. She opened her purse, dropped her cell phone inside, and stood. She was tall, with long brown hair.

"She's pretty," Dan commented.

"It runs in the family," Bowman informed him, and began walking toward the woman. Dan followed close behind.

When they met Bowman asked, "Angela?"

"Yes," she responded.

"Walter Bowman," he said, taking and shaking the hand she offered, and then turned. "This is Dan Coast. He helped me find you."

She took Dan's hand and said with a smile, "I owe you a great deal, Mr. Coast."

A woman across the park screamed.

Dan let go of Angela's hand.

Their heads turned toward the scream.

A man in a dark hooded sweatshirt and sunglasses stood five feet to Dan's right. He was holding a revolver. Bowman was between Dan and the gunman.

"Give me your purse!" the hooded man hollered.

Angela screamed as the man moved closer. He grabbed the purse with one hand and held the gun on Bowman and Dan with the other.

Bowman lunged at the gunman.

Dan tried to grab Bowman's arm to stop him, but it was too late. The gunman fired and Bowman doubled over, hitting the grass face first.

Dan froze and the thug turned the weapon on Angela, firing twice into her chest, and knocking her backwards to the ground.

He pointed the gun at Dan and paused. He quickly looked around the park at the other people. The woman that had screamed had fainted on the walking trail. He turned, and ran; disappearing into the trees.

Dan yanked his cell phone from his pocket and dropped to his knees beside Angela. "Hold on!" he said. He dialed 911. "This is Dan Coast. There's been a shooting in Bayview Park. Two people have been shot. Hurry!"

Dan dropped his phone and leaned over Angela. Blood pooled in her mouth and seeped down her chin. He pulled off his T-shirt and pressed it on the chest wounds.

A crowd was beginning to gather. Dan looked up at a man standing over him. "Hold this," Dan said. The man knelt down beside him and pressed firmly on the bullet holes.

Sirens began to wail in the distance.

Dan turned and crawled toward Bowman. When he reached him, he rolled him onto his back. He ripped open Bowman's shirt searching for entry wounds. There were none. He glanced down at Bowman's leg. His pant leg was wet with blood. He unbuckled Bowman's belt, yanking it through the belt loops, and quickly fashioned a tourniquet around Bowman's thigh.

"What happened?" Bowman mumbled.

"You've been shot," Dan replied. He glanced up at the first police cruiser hopping the curb and heading their way.

"Angela ... okay?" Bowman asked.

The officer leapt from his car and drew his weapon. He looked at Dan. "Are you hit?"

"No," Dan replied. "Her and him."

"The shooter?"

"He ran." Dan pointed in the direction of Truman Avenue.

The officer holstered his pistol and went to Angela. He crouched down beside her. Her eyes were wide. She coughed and blood spattered against the front of his shirt. "An ambulance is on its way, ma'am," he said. "Just hold on."

"Is Angela ... okay?" Bowman asked again.

Dan ignored the question and looked toward her.

The ambulance was driving across the park toward them.

Angela closed her eyes.

Chapter Twenty-Six

The elevator doors parted and Maxine could see Dan leaning with his back against the wall near the nurses station. He was biting his nails and staring into the floor, searching for an explanation of the day's events.

"Dan!" she called out as she ran toward him. "Thank God you're okay."

Dan pushed himself away from the wall and turned in her direction just as she threw her arms around him. "I'm fine, I'm fine! But you damn near knocked the breath out of me."

Maxine looked up at him. "What happened?"

"There was a man with a gun. He—"

"Is Walter alright?"

"He's in surgery now."

"His sister?" Maxine asked.

Dan shook his head no. "She didn't make it."

"Oh my God."

A doctor, dressed in blue scrubs, rounded the corner and made his way down the hall. He was muscular and stood a little over six feet tall. His mask dangled from its strings, around his neck. He removed his surgery cap to reveal his wavy blond hair. His chin, jaw, and cheek bones looked as if they had been chiseled from stone by Michelangelo himself. On his perfectly tanned face was two days growth of sexy stubble. "Mr. Coast?" he asked.

"Make it Dan."

They shook hands. "I'm Dr. Hans Mattsson. I performed the surgery on Mr. Bowman."

Mattsson's blue eyes shot to Maxine. "How are you, Maxine?"

"Good, Hans. How are you?"

A cocktail of emotions washed over Dan as Mattsson took Maxine's hand in his and held it for far too long. The message the Swede's thumb was conducting looked an awful lot like foreplay. Dan looked like smoke would come out of his ears at any moment. Maxine looked like she was about to climax.

Mattsson smiled back. Dan had seen the same grin once on a barracuda. A dead one

"It's been awhile," the doctor said.

Scowling, Dan looked from Maxine to Mattsson, and then back to Maxine.

"Yes, it has," Maxine agreed.

"Eh-hem!" Dan cleared his throat.

Maxine snapped out of her lust-induced stupor and let go of Mattsson's hand.

The smile left Mattsson's face. "I, uh … Mr. Bowman

is in recovery. He'll be moved into his room in a couple hours. We'll keep him overnight for observation."

"Can I see him?" Dan asked.

"Let's wait till he's in his room," Mattsson responded.

Maxine spoke up. "Dan has a few questions for him. Is there any way you can let him in now?"

Mattsson grinned. "Uh … yeah, why not. Maybe you and I can grab a cup of coffee in the cafeteria and catch up while Dan's in with Mr. Bowman."

"That's a great idea," Maxine said.

"Yeah, great idea," Dan grumbled.

The elevator doors opened again and Chief Rick Carver stepped into the hallway, his belly a good three seconds before the rest of him.

"Which way to recovery?" Dan asked.

Mattsson pointed in the opposite direction of the elevator. "Around the corner and through the double doors. He's in recovery room three."

"Can you hold Carver off for a while?" Dan asked.

"I think I can arrange that," Mattsson said.

"Thanks," said Dan, and walked down the hall.

Mattsson put his hand on the small of Maxine's back. "Shall we get that cup of coffee?"

Maxine looked over her shoulder and Dan glanced back just before he rounded the corner. Maxine smiled and winked.

Dan slowly pushed open the door of recovery room number three and peeked inside.

"Excuse me, sir," came a woman's voice from behind him. "May I help you?"

Dan turned and looked back across the hallway. Leaning against the wall was a large black woman in dark blue scrubs. Her arms were folded in front of her triple D bosom. She lowered one eyebrow and raised the other. "I said, 'May I help you?'"

Dan said, "I ... uh___"

"*I. Uh*," the woman mocked. "What's *I ... uh* mean?" She unfolded her arms and placed her hands on her hips and glared at Dan waiting for his answer.

"Dr. Mattsson told me it would be okay if I spoke with Mr. Bowman."

"Oh, he did, did he? Well, let *me* tell you something," she said, waving her finger in the air. "Dr. Mattsson doesn't run this unit. Reatha Davis runs this unit. You want to visit a patient in this unit, you march your skinny little white ass over here and you ask Mrs. Reatha *Davis* if you can talk to Mr. Bowman."

Dan let the door shut. "Okay." He looked up and down the hall. "Are you Reatha Davis?"

She widened her eyes and cocked her head. "Yes."

Dan took a deep breath. "Reath—"

"Mrs. Davis!" she scolded him.

"Mrs. Davis, can I—"

"*May* I!"

"May I speak with Mr, Bowman?"

She cocked her head even farther, waiting for more.

"Please."

"And you are?" Mrs. Davis asked.

"Dan Coast."

"Yes you may, Mr. Coast."

Dan pushed on the door. "Thank you."

"You're welcome, Mr. Coast."

Dan rolled his eyes as he walked through the door and mouthed the word "wow."

Walter Bowman lay in the hospital bed. An IV was attached to the back of his hand and wires ran into the neck hole of his gown. His eyes were closed.

"Walter," Dan whispered. He walked over and put his hand on Bowman's arm and gently squeezed. "Walter," he said a little louder.

Walter Bowman opened his eyes. He blinked a few times and looked around the room and then back at Dan. "Angela?" he asked, his voice a dry rasp.

"She didn't make it," Dan replied.

Bowman shut his eyes tightly. "Dammit."

When he opened his eyes again Dan asked, "Did you recognize the shooter?"

"No, never saw him before in my life. You?"

Dan shook his head no. "Didn't look familiar."

"How could this have happened?" Bowman asked.

"Did you tell anyone at all that we were meeting there?"

"I didn't tell anyone. I don't *know* anyone here." Bowman paused for a second. "Did she seem like she was in a lot of pain?"

"She didn't appear to be. She just looked confused."

"That makes two of us."

Dan patted Bowman's arm. "You get some rest. The doctor said they would be moving you into a regular room in a couple of hours. I'll stop back by this evening."

"Thanks, Coast."

Dan turned and made his way back through the door and into the hall. Reatha Davis sat at a desk in the nurses station. "You have a nice evening, Mr. Coast," she said smiling as he walked by.

Dan noticed that the nurse's demeanor had softened considerably. "You too, Mrs. Davis."

Dan walked into the cafeteria. Maxine and Dr. Wonderful were sitting at a table for two, next to the window, with a romantic view of the parking lot. Maxine sipped her coffee and laughed uproariously. Dan figured the doctor had either just told the greatest joke in comedy history or his awesome body was exuding a laughing gas-like pheromone. Dan made his way toward their table.

"Oh, Dan," Maxine said when she finally noticed him walking over. "How did everything go with Walter?"

"Wonderful," Dan replied. "Are you about done with your coffee, there?"

Maxine looked at the bottom of her cup. "I think so."

Dr. Mattsson stood and held out his hand. "It was nice to meet you, Dan."

Dan shook his hand. "You too."

Maxine got up from the table. "Thank you for the coffee, Hans. Next time it's on me."

They hugged and Mattsson said, "It's a deal."

As Maxine and Dan walked across the cafeteria floor Dan mumbled, "Next time?"

Maxine giggled. "Do I detect a bit of jealousy?"

"Jealous of what?"

"The most gorgeous doctor in the whole world," Maxine retorted.

"Wow, thanks for that," Dan said, as the two stepped onto the elevator. "And stop grinning like that. Christ! By the way, how is it that you and the Swedish meatball know each other?"

"Oh, Dan, we just know each other professionally. Remember, Key West's a small town. Live here long enough and you get to rub elbows with everyone eventually."

"And knock boots."

"I never said we knocked boots."

"But you'd like to."

Maxine's dreamy expression said she was thinking about it.

A look of panic spread over Dan's face. "The only boots you're knockin' are mine," he muttered as he whisked her through the exit.

Chapter Twenty-Seven

It was a little after five when Maxine backed her car into a parking spot at Red's Bar and Grill. Dan felt his phone vibrate as he climbed from the passenger seat. Charles Hamilton, the caller ID said.

"Crap!" Dan said.

"Whats the matter?" Maxine asked.

"Hamilton," Dan responded. "I'm supposed to meet him later."

"What's wrong with that?"

The couple made their way across the parking lot towards the front door. Dan looked up at the sun and wiped the sweat from his brow with the back of his hand and then repositioned his sunglasses with the tip of his index finger.

"He's probably already spoken with his wife and you can bet he's not very happy with me," he said.

Maxine thought about asking why but instead just

shrugged her shoulders. Dan pulled open the door and she walked in to the bar. She paused, waiting for her eyes to adjust to the darker room.

"Hey, you two!" Red called out.

Dan removed his sunglasses, hung them from the front of his shirt, and then ran into the back of Maxine who had stopped in front of him. "Really?" she said. "Slow down. The booze will still be there when you get to the bar."

Dan stepped around her. "Well, why did you stop in front of me like that?"

"I couldn't see."

"We'll get you a cane," Dan mumbled.

Red already had the tequila, Seven, and lime made and sitting on the bar when Dan reached his stool. He climbed aboard and Maxine joined him.

"What can I get you, Maxine?" Red asked.

Maxine thought for a second. "How about a margarita?"

"Coming right up." Red grabbed a margarita glass from the rack behind him and began making the drink. He turned his attention to Dan. "So, how did the family reunion turn out?"

Dan took a sip of his tequila. "One dead, one wounded."

Red froze. "What?"

"Some thug tried to grab Angela's purse. Bowman tried to stop it and the guy shot Bowman, then turned the gun on Angela."

"Oh my God! Who's dead?" Red asked.

"Bowman's sister," Dan replied. "She took two shots

to the chest."

"And Walter?"

"One in the leg. They're gonna keep him in the hospital overnight."

"How's he taking it?"

Dan shrugged. "I don't know. He seemed a little shook up when I spoke with him. I would imagine it hasn't really set in yet."

"Margarita," Maxine said, reminding Red of the task at hand.

"Oh, sorry," he answered, and resumed making the drink. When he was finished he sat the drink on the bar and slid it in front her. "Your highness," he said and pointedly performed a little bow.

"Just got a call from Charles Hamilton on our way in," Dan said matter-of-factly.

Red bugged out his eyes and showed his teeth in an attempt to show over-exaggerated fear. "What did he have to say?" he asked.

"I didn't answer the phone."

"I don't blame ya. I bet he's pretty pissed."

Dan laughed. "I bet."

"What did you two do?" Maxine inquired. "Or shouldn't I ask?"

"We sold the pictures to Hamilton's wife and tonight we're gonna sell the copies to Hamilton," Dan explained.

"Isn't that against the law?" Maxine asked.

"So is kicking the shit out of someone in their own bar," Red answered, rubbing his aching ribs.

Dan's phone vibrated. He reached for it and glanced at

the call screen. "Speak of the devil."

"You gonna answer it?" Red asked.

"Let's see if he leaves a message." The call ended and Dan stared at the screen. When a small number one appeared next to the voicemail icon he said. "He did."

Dan tapped the icon and then hit the speaker button. "Coast! This is Charles Hamilton!" screamed Hamilton's voice from the speaker. "You better answer your goddamn phone!"

"He's mad alright," Maxine pointed out.

Red looked around the room at a few of the patrons who were looking toward the bar. A few were grinning, and a couple were annoyed. "Sorry folks," he said, pointing at Dan's phone. "Wrong number."

Hamilton's angry voice continued. "If you don't call me back right away, I'll make sure you're never able to dial another phone as long as you live." *Click!*

"That's an odd threat," Dan said. "If he breaks my fingers how can I call him back?"

"Maybe he's going to cut them off," Maxine suggested.

"Either way, I don't really like being threatened," said Dan. "We better set up a meeting for tonight."

"We?" Red asked. "Does that mean *we* have to drive all the way back to Key Largo?"

"Don't be ridiculous. We'll make him come to us."

Red turned and looked at the clock over the back bar. "When will this meeting take place … and where?"

"I don't know. How about if you give me a ride back over to the hospital in a bit to talk with Bowman? I want to find out what the cops asked him, and what they told him."

Double Trouble

"I can do that," Red replied. "Cindy should be here any minute."

Maxine finished her margarita and pushed the empty glass across the bar. "And I'll have another margarita," she said.

The three sat and talked and a short time later Cindy walked through the door. "Hi guys," she said, when she got to the bar. She reached under the counter and pulled out an apron and tied it around her waist. "What's on the agenda for tonight?" She walked behind the bar and began filling the sink with hot water.

Red said, "You're in charge tonight. I have to help Dan with something."

Maxine sipped her drink. "I only have one thing on my agenda, and that's to sit here on this stool and drink margaritas."

"Good," Cindy giggled. "You can keep me company while these old farts are out doing whatever it is that old farts do on a Tuesday evening."

"Ouch," Dan and Red said in unison.

"Sounds like a plan," Maxine laughed. "It's not often I get to carry on a conversation with someone close to my own age."

"Double ouch," Dan winced. "Maybe Dr. Wonderful will show up and you can buy him that drink."

"Ooh, maybe," Maxine jabbed.

"I'm guessing there's a good story *there*," Cindy said.

"An *amazing* story," Maxine corrected, her eyes wide. "We'll talk about it when these two leave."

Dan shook his head in discouragement as he climbed from his bar stool.

157

Maxine puckered her lips. "Don't forget to kiss me good bye," she sang out.

Dan leaned in and kissed her.

"Be careful," Maxine said seriously.

Dan grinned. "Always."

Red walked around the bar and headed for the door. "Come on, ya old fart."

"That's enough of the old fart talk, Red," Dan said. "Oh, by the way, did I tell you I'm having dinner with Kip Larson Friday night?"

"Who the hell is Kip Larson?"

Chapter Twenty-Eight

Red pulled his Firebird off of College Road and into the parking lot of The Lower Keys Medical Center.

"Sorry, I've never heard of Kip Larson," he apologized after Dan had gone on and on about his upcoming meeting with the NASA legend.

Dan wanted to scream. "Unbelievable! Have you ever heard of Neil Armstrong or Buzz Aldrin?" he said as he and Red climbed from the car.

"Well, yeah. They're famous astronauts."

Dan lightly pounded his head against the car's roof. "So is Kip Larson. Christ!"

"Maybe you should donate some money to this building so we can get a better parking spot next time," Red noted as the two walked across the hot blacktop toward the building.

Dan just mumbled "Famous astronauts" under his breath.

Dan and Red stepped off the elevator and went straight to the main nurses station.

"We're looking for Walter Bowman's room," Dan said.

The nurse behind the counter went to a blue clipboard lying on top of the desk and flipped through the pages. "Room six, straight down this hall to your right."

"Thanks," said Dan.

The door was propped open and they went inside. Walter had the head of his bed raised slightly. His arms were folded behind his head and he was watching Wheel of Fortune. "Hey, guys," he said as they entered.

"How ya feeling?" Dan asked.

Bowman unlocked his fingers from behind his head and straightened his blankets. "I feel fine. I don't know why they won't let me leave today. I just want to get off this island and put all this behind me."

"I don't blame you," Red said as he gazed at the television. "A stitch in time saves nine!" he shouted.

Dan turned to look at the TV screen.

A stitch in time saves nine, the contestant said.

"Yes!" Red cried with a celebratory fist pump.

Dan turned back to Bowman. "Did you talk to the police?"

"Yeah, Chief Carver was here, and an investigator—Tripp, I think his name was. They also had a woman do a sketch of the shooter, from my description."

"What kind of things did the investigator ask you?" Dan asked.

"How we found Angela, did anyone else know we were meeting at the park, did I recognize the shooter, basic

160

questions like that."

"You're sure you didn't tell anyone?"

"Hollywood Walk of Fame!" Red hollered.

Dan flinched. "Stop that. Christ!"

"I swear, I didn't tell anyone," Bowman vowed.

"Did they leave a copy of the sketch?" Dan asked.

Bowman glanced at the bedside stand. "Yes. I stuck it in the drawer."

Dan opened the drawer, looked at the sketch, folded it, and shoved it in his pocket.

Hollywood Walk of Fame, one of the contestants guessed.

"Yes," Red whispered.

Dan shot him a look.

"What?" Red asked.

"Don't worry, Bowman," Dan said. "We'll get this guy."

Bowman responded, "Dan, you've already done enough. You said you would find my sister and you did. As soon as I get back to my hotel room I'll write you a check for the balance of your services."

"You don't want me to keep going?" Dan asked.

"Just let the police handle it. It's their job."

Dan shrugged. "If that's what you want, Bowman."

Bowman pointed toward the closet. "Actually, there is one more thing you can do for me."

"What's that?"

"My car keys are in a clear plastic bag in the closet.

161

Can you pick up the Lincoln and park it at your house tonight?"

Dan started for the closet. "Sure, I can do that."

"Thanks. I'll pick it up tomorrow when they spring me."

"I can pick you up here tomorrow and give you a ride back to your hotel if you want," Dan offered.

"Sure, that would be great. Thanks."

Dan opened the bag, pulled out the keys and stuffed them in his pocket. "We're gonna head out. Give me a call in the morning when you find out what time you get out of here."

"Will do," Bowman replied.

Dan walked out into the hallway. "Come on, Red."

Red was still engrossed in the television. He put up his hand. "Hold on."

"All Roads Lead To Rome Wasn't Built In A Day!" Bowman shouted.

"Bastard!" Red yelled.

Chapter Twenty-Nine

"So, where is the thumb drive?" Red asked. He pulled into a spot next to Bowman's rental car.

"In my pocket," Dan answered. He opened the door and climbed out.

"Are you going to drop Bowman's car at your house and I'll pick you up?"

"Why don't you park *your* car at your house and we'll take the Lincoln," Dan suggested.

"Good idea," Red agreed.

Dan jumped into the Town Car, backed it out, and drove down the street. He took a right on Virginia Street. Red followed close behind in the Firebird.

Dan inspected the interior of the car as he drove toward Red's house. He knew he would soon be buying himself a new car, and he wondered if the Lincoln Town Car was the car for him. He ran the palm of his hand along the dashboard, then he reached down and turned on the radio. The radio was tuned to Radio Margaritaville. *Good*

Man, Dan thought. Jimmy Buffett and Old Blue Eyes duetting on "Mack the Knife." Dan turned it up, and then lowered the front windows. He put his arm out the window and tapped the door to the beat.

Dan pulled to the curb in front of Red's house and Red pulled into his driveway.

By the time Red got out of his car and got into the Lincoln, Ziggy Marley was singing "Love is My Religion."

"Great song," Red said, shutting the car door. "Love is my religion, too."

Dan snorted. "Yeah, right. Sex, money, and booze are your religion."

"Pot calling the kettle black."

Dan's cell phone rang. It was Charles Hamilton. "Yeah," Dan said.

"I'm here. Where the hell are you?" Hamilton asked.

"Be there in a second," Dan replied, and put the car in drive.

"Someone a little impatient?" Red asked.

"Rich people think they're not supposed to wait for anyone or anything."

"How come you don't act like that?"

"I meant normal rich people."

Dan pulled off of Roosevelt into the Winn-Dixie parking lot. It was well lit and there were a lot of people around.

"What does he drive?" Red asked.

"I have no idea," Dan replied.

"How will we find him?"

Dan searched the parking lot. "He said he would be wearing a pink carnation."

"Really?"

"No, not really. I *know* what he looks like." Dan made a loop and on the second time around he spotted Hamilton standing next to a black Mercedes. Pointing, he said, "There he is."

Dan parked in a spot two rows behind Hamilton and they got out of the car.

"Did you bring a gun?" Red asked.

"For what?" Dan replied.

"In case the shit hits the fan."

"There's no shit, and there's no fan. We're going to give him the thumb drive and he's going to give us five grand."

"Five grand? I thought he was paying you five *hundred* for this."

"He was, but then you got the shit kicked out of you, Maxine was followed, and my dog was run over. I think he's getting off cheap."

"I guess you're right."

"Hamilton," Dan said as they walked up behind him.

Hamilton spun around; he did not look happy. "Dammit, Coast, I've been waiting here for a half hour."

"Sorry, we were visiting a friend in the hospital."

"That's where you're going to end up if you don't hand over those photographs," Hamilton threatened.

Dan reached into his pocket and pulled out the thumb drive. "You got the five grand?"

Hamilton turned and pulled open the passenger side

door. He reached in and retrieved a large manila envelope, sealed and folded to the size of a stack of bills, off of the front seat.

Dan nodded his head toward Red and Hamilton handed Red the envelope. Red unfolded the envelope and ripped off the top. He looked inside. "Looks like it's all here."

"Of course it's all there," Hamilton said angrily. "Now that makes twenty thousand dollars you've made off of this job."

Dan handed the thumb drive to Hamilton. "It was nice doing business with you," he said with a grin.

Hamilton yanked it from his fingers. "It *will* be the last time. I could have your license for this, Coast. I'm a very powerful man, you know."

Dan chuckled. "I hear what you're saying, Hamilton, and I think you might even believe it. But if I had a dollar for every powerful man I've overpowered—"

"—He'd have about three dollars," Red inserted.

Dan shot Red a glance. "Maybe four," he corrected, and then returned his attention to Hamilton. Dan closed the short distance between himself and Hamilton and through clenched teeth he whispered, "Powerful men may be loud and full of threats, but a man who has nothing to lose will put a bullet in your skull just for fun."

Charles Hamilton's eyes widened and he stepped back. He remained silent as he walked around the car, got in, and sped away.

Red handed the envelope full of money to Dan. "Put a bullet in your skull just for fun," said Red. "A little harsh don't you think?"

Dan laughed as he turned and headed back to the car. "I heard that line in an old movie once. Never thought I would get to use it. Sounded pretty cool, didn't it?"

"Pretty cool," Red agreed. "But my question is, what license was he going to take? You don't have a PI license. You don't even have a driver's license."

Dan shrugged his shoulders. "Who knows? Maybe he was gonna go after my fishing license."

Chapter Thirty

Dan Coast walked out of the bathroom of his room at the Casa Marina Resort. He was wearing running shorts and a dark green T-shirt that read MILLER'S MILLS SUNDAE RUN across the front.

Dan's wife, Alex sat on the bed, bent over, and tying her running shoes. "Can you imagine running here every morning, after we move?" she asked. "It's just so beautiful. I still can't believe it."

"We'll have to run a little later than this, though, because after we move here I'm throwing this watch in a drawer and I'm never setting another alarm clock."

"Sounds like a good plan," Alex agreed.

Dan slipped his feet into his running shoes and knelt down to tie them. He fumbled with the laces.

"Come on," Alex said. "Hurry up."

Dan folded the shoelace to make a loop. *Around the back and through the loop*, he thought. *Why is this so hard to do?*

"Hurry up!" Alex said angrily. "I have to go."

"I know, I know. I'm trying."

"Hurry!"

"I'm trying. I just can't seem to remember how to—"

"I have to go. If you don't come with me, you have to stay here, by yourself." Alex reached down and grabbed Dan's hand. "Please, come with me."

"I can't!" Dan shouted.

Alex let go of his hand and walked toward the door. "I have to go."

"Please!" Dan cried out. "Please don't go. Don't leave me."

The door slammed shut behind her and startled Dan awake.

*****

Dan rolled over in bed. *Dammit!* he thought, as he looked around the room. The ceiling fan spun on low above him, the sunshine beamed through his bedroom window. He rubbed his eyes and then reached for his cell phone. No one had called. He pulled back the covers and swung his feet to the floor. He glanced at the clock on the nightstand. 7:15.

Maxine had left Red's the night before and stayed at her place and Dan was in bed early, for once ... and sober. He couldn't remember the last time he woke up this early without an alarm. The rare mornings he woke up feeling good always made him wonder why he drank at all. But deep down inside he knew. The more you drink the less you dream.

He stood and walked naked to the bathroom. After he peed, he turned on the cold water and splashed some on his face. Dan stared at himself in the mirror, then sucked in his gut, and flexed his pecs. He flexed his biceps. *Seen worse*, he thought, and returned to his bedroom.

Opening his dresser drawer, he searched through his T-shirts. When he came to the one he was looking for he pulled it out and put it on. BOILERMAKER 15K ROAD RACE, it said, in blue letters. He grabbed a pair of gym shorts and slipped them on, and then went to the closet to find his sneakers.

He walked out his back door and when he got to the bottom of the steps he turned, put his toes against the bottom step, and pushed, stretching his calf muscle. When he finished that he bent and tried to touch his toes. *Not even close*, he thought. Dan stretched his thighs and hamstrings, then stretched his arms over his head, reaching toward the clear blue sky.

He heard Bev's back door slam shut, and when he turned around she was leaning against the railing with her palms on the top rail. "Someone better check the temperature in hell this morning," she said, "because it could be snowing."

Dan had hoped to get away before anyone saw him. "I thought maybe I would try to get back into it," he said.

"I thought maybe you had gone insane."

Dan waved her off, turned, and jogged toward the beach. Not only was this the first time he had run since moving to Key West, it was also the first time he was going to run without Alex at his side. He looked toward Smathers Beach, and then turned and gazed in the other direction. Either way he looked, the white sand beaches stretched toward their vanishing points.

Undaunted, Dan took a deep breath and began running. When he came to the first access path he turned and ran up onto Atlantic Boulevard. He took a right at White Street and then a left at Casa Marina Court Inn. When he got to the end of the street he stopped and stared up at the Casa Marina in all it's majestic glory. He remembered their last run together like it was only yesterday.

Leaning over, Dan put his hands on his knees. His heart was pounding. He didn't know if it was from the run or from the memories. "Why?" he whispered. "Why did you have to leave me?"

Dan Coast turned and began his walk home.

Chapter Thirty-One

After showering and shaving Dan made coffee. He drank two cups with his blueberry Pop-Tarts, the kind with no frosting, and then jumped in Bowman's Lincoln and headed for the animal hospital.

"How ya doing, pal?" Dan asked his dog when he entered the room.

Buddy jumped to his feet. He looked a lot better than he had the day before.

Dr. Lee came into the room through another door. "He's doing great, Mr. Coast."

"I guess so," Dan said, as he scratched Buddy's head.

"They're not big babies, like people," Dr. Lee remarked. "Much more resilient."

"Will I be able to take him home today, Doc?" Dan asked.

Lee glanced up at the clock on the wall. "Why don't you come back around five, just before we close. That way

I'll be able to watch him eat and go to the bathroom a few more times. I just want to make sure he's not too uncomfortable."

Dan rubbed Buddy's back near the tail, which never failed to make the dog flick his tongue in ecstasy. "Sounds like a good idea. I have to do a couple things this afternoon anyway."

Dr. Lee shook Dan's hand and Dan thanked him for the millionth time before leaving.

When Dan returned to the car he thought about calling Maxine, but then dialed Walter Bowman's cell phone instead. Bowman's voice mail picked up so Dan hit the end call button. He looked down at the time on the dashboard. It was nine-thirty, so he decided to drive out to the hospital.

Dan pulled the black Lincoln Town Car off of College Road and into the parking lot of the Lower Keys Medical Center, parked, and went inside. He rode the elevator up to Bowman's floor and went directly to his room.

Dan pushed open the door to Bowman's room. "Hey, you about ready to get out of this joint?" Bowman's bed was empty and had been made up. Dan went to the bathroom door and knocked. "Bowman?" he called out, and then knocked again. He reached down and pulled open the door; there was no one inside.

Leaving the room, Dan walked across the hall to the nurse's station. "Can I help you?" a young nurse asked. She was sitting at the desk eating a bacon, egg, and cheese croissant from McDonald's, and sipping a cup of coffee.

"Walter Bowman," Dan said. "He's not in his room."

The woman reached over and grabbed a file folder out of a bin next to the computer. "Are you a relative?" she asked.

"Yeah," Dan replied.

The nurse opened the folder and scanned the first page. "Mr. Bowman checked himself out last night."

Dan lowered his brow. "Last night? What time?"

She glanced back at the paperwork. "Ten o'clock."

As Dan turned and walked toward the elevator he heard a snotty "You're welcome" from the nurse. He whirled and said, "Oh, did I forget to say thanks for your half-ass help?" The woman spluttered a garbled obscenity, nearly choking on her croissant, as she watched the elevator doors slide shut.

While Dan walked across the parking lot he dialed Bowman's number again; it went to voice mail. "Bowman. Dan Coast. Give me a call when you get this message."

As Dan drove down Flagler Avenue he called Rick Carver.

"Carver."

"Rick. It's Dan."

Carver let out a sigh. "I knew my day was going far too well."

"Rick, have you heard from Walter Bowman this morning," Dan asked.

"Yeah. He was in here about an hour ago. Why?"

"He checked himself out of the hospital last night, and he won't answer his cell or return my calls."

"So?"

"Doesn't that seem a little strange?"

"No. He got a call last night that his father had passed away," Rick explained. "He wanted to get his brother's body released from the morgue and get back to Seattle.

Besides, I rarely return your calls either."

"Did you release the body?"

"Yes."

"To which funeral home?"

Rick moved around some papers on his desk. "Legro and Arnt over on Olivia Street."

"If someone brought you a fingerprint, how long would it take to find out the person's identity?"

"All depends. If they're in the system, it could take five minutes to get a match, or it could take three hours."

"Rick, I really need your help on this one. I'm gonna have Maxine bring you two glasses. One has my prints on it—not sure which one. I need you to run the set of prints from the second glass. Can you do that for me?"

"Sure, Coast. It's a slow day. And you know how much I like being your toady."

"Thanks," Dan said, and hung up the phone. Then he dialed Maxine's number.

"Hello?"

"Maxine, it's Dan."

"I know."

"Where are you?"

"On my way to your house."

"I need a favor. Remember the two glasses in the sink you were going to wash the other night?"

"Yes."

"I need you to put them in two different bags and bring them to Rick Carver at the police station, he's expecting you. And Maxine, try not to touch the outside of the glasses. Handle them with a dishcloth or something."

"Okay. I'm pulling into your driveway now."

"Thanks, Maxine. Bye."

Dan drove almost to the end of Olivia Street and parked in front of the Legro and Arnt Funeral Home. Inside he approached a woman vacuuming the floor. He touched her shoulder and she jumped.

"Sorry. I didn't mean to scare you," Dan said. "I'm looking for someone."

The woman smiled and said, "No speak, English."

Dan looked around the room. "Is there somebody here who can help me?"

"I can help you."

Dan turned to see a very tall and very thin man approaching him. He was dressed in a black suit, with a black tie, and a white shirt. He had a somber look on his gray, wrinkled face. The man held out his hand and when Dan grabbed it to shake the man's fingers wrapped almost completely around Dan's hand. He reminded Dan of John Carradine, the old horror film actor.

"I'm looking for someone," Dan repeated.

The man still held Dan's hand in his. "Who are you looking for?"

Dan wiggled his hand out of the man's grip. "Walter Bowman. I was told his brother's body was released to you this morning."

"Yes, yes it was."

"If you're here to pay your respects, I'm sorry, the body has already been sent out."

"Sent out where?" Dan asked.

"The crematorium."

"How long ago?"

"Maybe a half hour."

"Where is that located?"

"On Truman Avenue. If you can wait a second I can get the exact address for you."

"I'll find it. Thank you," Dan said and left.

Dan pulled up in front of the Florida Keys Crematory and threw the car into park. The front door was locked so Dan pushed the buzzer and waited. A short pudgy man wearing an almost exact replica of the funeral director's suit pushed open the door. With his bulging eyes, full lips, and slicked-back hair, Dan thought he was a dead ringer for Peter Lorre, another horror great.

"Can I help you?" the man said. Even his creepy, high-pitched voice was Lorre-esque.

Dan fought off an involuntary shudder and managed to say, "I'm looking for a Walter Bowman. I believe his brother Warren might be here."

The odd little man pushed the door open farther. "Yes, he is. Come on in."

"Thank you," Dan said, and walked inside.

Dan followed the man to a small wooden table. Draped with a blue velvet tablecloth. Sitting atop it was an antique brass urn. The man stopped and pointed. "Here's Mr. Bowman."

Dan stared at the urn. "You mean he's already been cremated?"

"Why, yes. We did it right away."

"Do you always do them that quick?"

"Special circumstances."

"How much extra did he give you?"

A look of outrage played upon the man's face. "That's *no*t how we do business here. I'll have to ask you to leave, sir."

Dan grabbed the elf by his shoulders and effortlessly hoisted him to eye level. "I said, *how much*?"

Pudgy looked frantically around the room, as if a corpse might overhear, and whispered, "Five thousand dollars."

Dan set him down. "What time is he supposed to return to pick up the ashes?"

"Oh, he's not. We're shipping them to Seattle for him."

"How long ago did he leave here?"

"About ten minutes before you arrived."

Chapter Thirty-Two

Dan Coast pulled up in front of The Atlantic Inn Hotel. A young valet in a black jacket hurried to the car. "Good morning Mr. Coast," the valet said. "New car?"

"It's not my car, Billy," Dan replied. "I borrowed it from a friend and I'm returning it to him. He's staying here. Can you look up a room number for me?"

"If I was inside I could, but there's no way to do that from out here, Mr. Coast."

"It's Dan, Billy."

"I know, Mr. Coast, but I got yelled at last time my boss heard me call you Dan."

"I'll have a word with him," Dan joked.

"Please don't."

Dan slapped Billy on the back as he passed him. "Tell your mom I said hi."

"I will Mr. Coast, and Dan—"

Dan paused and turned back. "Yeah, Billy?"

"Thanks for the help with my tuition … and everything else."

Dan put his finger to his lips. "Shhh."

Dan entered the lobby and scouted the room for a familiar face. Across the room, dressed in white capris and a blue Hawaiian shirt, he spotted him and walked over.

The young man turned and put a hand to his chest. "Daniel Coast!" he screeched. "It's been a while. Haven't laid eyes on you since your Christmas party, I believe. That's far too long to go without a glimpse of your handsome face."

"Um, yeah. I need you to do something for me, Michael."

Michael shook his head. "Mmm, mmm, mmm. You have no idea what I could do for you, Daniel."

"Yeah, well, that's real flattering, Michael, but for now I just need you to look up a room number for me."

Michael pushed out his bottom lip and made a sad face. "Okay. For you, I'll do it. But you know it's against the rules and I'm putting my career on the line for you only because we are such good friends."

"Well, thank you. I really appreciate it."

Michael turned and made his way to the check-in desk. He jumped behind one of the keyboards. "What's the name, Daniel?"

"Walter Bowman."

"Walter Bowman," Michael repeated, and began punching keys. "I don't like him. Very rude man. And that friend of his—"

"Friend?"

"Yes. Very menacing. Scary, even"

Dan pulled the composite drawing from his pocket, unfolded it and laid it on the desk. "Does he look like this?"

"Not at all."

"I didn't think so. Is his friend staying here, also?"

"No."

"What room is Bowman in?"

"He's on the third floor, room 306. Anything else?" Michael asked with a wink.

"That'll do it," said Dan and he turned toward the elevator.

Dan strolled down the hallway until he came to 306. He knocked on the door and placed his thumb over the peephole. "Housekeeping," he said in a falsetto voice, hoping it would sound convincingly female.

"No thank you," Bowman called out from inside the room.

"Housekeeping," Dan repeated.

"I said no thank you! I'm checking out. You can come back and clean then."

"Housekeeping."

"Oh for crying out loud." Bowman yanked open the door.

"Were you going to leave without saying good bye?" Dan asked.

Bowman was surprised to see him. "Dan! I was just going to call you." He stepped aside and Dan walked into the room.

Dan made his way across the floor to the sliding glass

doors. "Nice room," he commented. Dan slid open the door and walked out on to the balcony. "Great view." Dan glanced down at the swimming pool three floors below him.

Bowman dug through a black leather bag that sat on the bed. "Let me find my checkbook and I'll pay you."

"That would be great," Dan said.

"But then you'll have to excuse me. I have a flight to catch."

"Are you flying your brother's body back, also?"

"No. The funeral home will ship it."

"The ashes, you mean."

"Um … yeah, the ashes. I had him cremated." Bowman found the checkbook. "Can never find a pen when you need one," he said, his voice shaky.

Dan felt his phone vibrate in his pocket. He pulled it out and looked at the screen. "Excuse me, Bowman. I have to take this call."

"No problem." Bowman found a pen and began writing.

"Hello," Dan said. "Yes … yes … okay … okay … I won't … bye." Dan placed the phone back in his pocket.

"Here you go," Bowman said, handing Dan the check.

Dan held the check in front of him, inspecting it, and said, "Oops, I think you made a mistake."

"Oh, did I put the wrong date?"

"Nope," Dan said handing it back to him. "The wrong name."

Bowman grinned nervously. "What … what do you

mean?"

"That was Chief Carver on the phone. They ran your prints from the glass you drank out of at my house. They came back a match for *Warren* Bowman." Dan took the sketch out of his pocket, unfolded it, and threw it on the bed. "I wondered how the sketch could end up looking nothing like the guy. I mean, to me these sketches don't look like the bad guy very often, but the guy that shot your sister didn't even have facial hair. You had them draw a full beard."

"I had to steer them in the wrong direction," Bowman confessed.

"The cops are on their way," Dan informed him.

"I could run for it."

"You could, but I can probably run faster."

"Can you run faster than a bullet, Coast?" Bowman's accomplice said as he entered the room. The same gun that killed Angela Breck was now pointed at Dan's head.

"Probably not," Dan said.

"Dan, I would like you to meet a good friend of mine, Mr. Albert Bunch," Bowman said. "We spent some time together at a minimum security facility in Washington. Mr. Bunch is what I like to call a handyman."

"I think the more common term is murderer," Dan said.

"Yes, but not only is he good at killing people, he's also good at causing automobile accidents," Bowman said, and laughed.

"Like the one your parents were in," Dan said.

"I should have shot him in the park," Bunch said. "Grab your things, Bowman, let's get out of here. But first, maybe I should waste this mother."

Dan gulped. "If you don't mind, this mother would rather you didn't."

"You leave us no choice, Coast," said Bowman. "As they say in the movies, you know too much."

"Yeah, I guess I do. The only thing that doesn't make sense is why your brother was buried in my back yard."

"We almost screwed up there, Coast," Bowman admitted. "It was my brother who originally wanted to hire you. I didn't. We fought about it, and I killed him right there on the beach. Then I panicked and tried to bury him. When I heard you coming down the trail with that damn dog of yours, I ran. I called Albert, and when you and your little girlfriend went back in the house, we took the body."

"Then why did you go ahead and hiring me?"

"It didn't take long to see what a drunken, bumbling moron you were. I thought it would look good if I hired a private investigator. I sure didn't think it would hurt."

"I guess you were wrong," Dan said. "I'm not as stupid as you thought."

"Really, Dan? I don't hear any sirens yet. You didn't tell the authorities where you were, did you?"

Shit! Dan thought, as Albert Bunch raised his weapon.

Dan jammed his fingertips under one of the suitcases on the bed and hurled it at Bunch. He turned and ran for the sliding glass doors, when he reached the end of the carpet he threw out his arms and jumped.

Bunch fired three times.

As Dan cleared the railing he felt a stinging in his thigh. He screamed all the way to the pool.

As he pulled himself out of the water he could hear the approaching sirens, as well as the screams of the hotel guests around and in the pool.

Dan crawled up on the cement skirting and collapsed. He looked back at the blood in the water and then down at his leg. He rolled on to his back and everything went dark.

*****

"Dan … Dan. You okay?"

Dan Coast slowly opened his eyes just as someone slapped his cheek. He was on his back, looking up at the dark figure silhouetted in the glare of the sunlight.

"What happened?" Dan asked.

An onlooker stepped in front of the sun and Dan saw that it was Rick Carver who was kneeling over him. "They said you jumped off the balcony," Rick informed him. "Damn lucky you hit in the deep end."

"My leg … he shot me."

"It's just a scratch," Rick said. "You must have caught your leg on something when you went over the railing."

"Where's Bowman?" Dan asked. "And the other guy, Albert Bunch? He was the shooter at the park."

Rick pulled off his gold-rimmed aviator sunglasses. "They got away. We didn't get here in time."

"Aw, Christ! Really?"

"No, not really, ya dumb ass. They're both in custody. Now get your ass up, there's nothing wrong with you." Carver stood and reached down to take Dan's hand. Dan grabbed it and Carver pulled him to his feet.

"Real funny," Dan said.

"I thought so." Rick turned and started toward his

patrol car. "Come on. Let's get to the station so someone can take your statement."

Dan grabbed Carver's shoulder. Carver turned around. "Rick," Dan said somberly. "I'm sorry about the way I acted back at Christmas time—ya know, calling you a fat bastard, the DWI, and all. I hope we can get past all that."

Rick held out his hand and they shook. "Don't worry about it."

Chapter Thirty-Three

Maxine steered her Ford Focus into Dan's driveway and shut off the engine. Dan swung open the passenger side door and pulled the seat forward. Buddy slowly climbed out of the back seat.

"Ya need some help there, pal?" Dan asked.

Buddy went directly to one of the palm trees in the front yard, hiked his leg, and re-marked his territory. After he finished he walked down the gravel path that led to the backyard and down to the two Adirondack chairs next to the fire pit. He surveyed the property as he walked along, taking it all in as though he had been gone for years.

"Looks like he's glad to be back," Maxine commented. She and Dan followed Buddy to the backyard and watched as he lay down next to one of the chairs.

"Guess he just wants to take a nap," said Dan. "Maybe I'll join him." Dan walked over and sat down. Buddy scooted his body over so his side was touching Dan's leg. Dan reached down and touched his head.

Maxine said, "I'm going to fill up his water dish and bring it out so he doesn't have to walk all the way to the house for a drink."

"Great idea. Can you bring me out a tequila, Seven, and lime dish, so *I* don't have to walk all the way to the house for a drink? After all, I did just survive a thirty-foot fall."

Maxine went through the back door shaking her head and returned a few minutes later with a drink for Buddy and also one for Dan. "Bev said you went for a run this morning."

"Bev has a big mouth."

Maxine handed Dan his drink. "How did you do?"

"I came in first place."

"Maybe we could run together tomorrow morning."

Dan rubbed his thigh. "Not with this leg injury, and I also have a lot of yard work to do." He took a sip of his drink.

"It's just a scratch, and you know you won't do any yard work." Maxine sat down in the other Adirondack chair.

"You're probably right."

"So, what's next?"

"What do you mean?"

"Well, you closed both of your cases. What's next on the agenda?"

"Nothing … nothing at all. I'm going to do nothing for the next few weeks. Maybe go fishing, sit in the backyard and drink tequila, and read the newspaper. Go to dinner with Kip Larson. I'm going to sleep late every morning. Do nothing and relax."

"Oh, that's what I was supposed to tell you, Bev said Kip had to go out of town. Dinner with your childhood hero will have to wait until next weekend."

"Dammit!" Dan felt his phone vibrate and took it out of his pocket. "Who's this?" he asked himself, as he stared at the caller ID. "Hello?"

"Dan Coast?"

"That's me."

"Mr. Coast, this is Reatha Davis ... from the hospital. I got your number from a co-worker."

"Oh, yeah. What do you want?"

"Mr. Coast, the man my husband works for was found dead this morning," Reatha Davis explained, near tears.

Dan sipped his drink. "Well, I didn't do it."

"I don't have time for smartasses, Mr. Coast. You shut up and listen!"

"That's the Reatha Davis I know. Go on."

"They arrested my husband. They think he killed him. Mr. Coast, can you help me?"

"Mrs. Davis, it's w*ill* I help you."

The End

COMING SPRING 2016
Jake Stellar
When Death Returns

ALSO BY RODNEY RIESEL

Sleeping Dogs Lie

From the Tales of Dan Coast

A mystery set in the Florida Keys follows Dan Coast, an unlicensed private detective of sorts, as he is hired to find the missing boyfriend of a woman who herself soon ends up missing. When someone from the woman's past unexpectedly shows up at Dan's home, with a story of faked deaths and missing life insurance money; Dan along with his sidekick Red set out to find the money, and the woman.

ISBN: 978-0-9883503-0-4

Ocean Floors

From the Tales of Dan Coast

The second installment in the Dan Coast series, Ocean Floors, is a tale of mystery and possible romance when a chance meeting with a beautiful young woman leads Dan and his trusted sidekick Red down a road of murder and kidnapping. Join Dan and Red as they try to solve the murder while searching for a missing friend.

ISBN: 978-0-9894877-0-2

Impaled

An Adirondack Short Story

Eric Stone is an investigator with The Town of Webb
Police Department. Chuck Little is Head Ranger at the
Nick's Lake campground. An unlikely duo, together they
work to solve a murder that mimics a spree of gruesome
murders taking place years earlier. Is it a copycat, or has
the murderer resurfaced after all of these years? Join Stone
and Little as they piece together the clues to solve this
mystery taking place in the small village of Old Forge in
the Adirondack Mountains.

North Murder Beach

A Jake Stellar Novel

The first installment of the story of North Myrtle Beach
police detective, Jake Stellar. The spring bike rallies have
ended, the spring breakers have all gone back to school,
and the summer tourist season is a few weeks away. What
better time for a police officer to take a nice quiet relaxing
week off from work? That's what Jake Stellar had in mind.
That is until someone from his past resurfaces to remind
him of a terrible secret he has spent years trying to forget.
In North Murder Beach, a story of revenge, Jake is
unwillingly and violently forced to confront his secret
from his past.

ISBN: 978-0-9894877-1-9

The Coast of Christmas Past

From the Tales of Dan Coast

Coast of Christmas Past is the third book in the Dan Coast series of books. Dan Coast is all set to spend Christmas just the same way he has every year for the past few years; alone and drunk. But when uninvited, unexpected guests arrive and throw a wrench into his holiday plans he is forced to sober up (slightly), and throw on a smile. Just when it seems nothing else could go wrong, a close friend is injured in what appears, to the police, to be a drug deal gone bad. Dan Coast and his sidekick, Red jump into action to find the truth while their friend lies unconscious in the hospital.

ISBN: 978-0-9894877-3-3

The Man in Room Number Four

The Dunquin Cove Series

When a mysterious stranger arrives in the small coastal town of Dunquin Cove, Maine it appears as though Claire and her young son, Mica's prayers have been answer.

But who is he, and why is he really here? Join Claire and her guests at the Colsome House Bed and Breakfast as they piece together the mystery of the Man in Room Number Four.

ISBN: 978-0-9894877-2-6

Ship of Fools

From the Tales of Dan Coast

Ship of Fools is the fourth book in The Tales of Dan Coast series and begins where Coasts of Christmas Past left off. Find out how Dan deals with the death of a young friend, while looking into the disappearance of a new friend's sister. Join Dan, Red, and Skip as they fumble their way through a new mystery.

ISBN: 978-0-9894877-4-0

Beach Shoot

A Jake Stellar Series

It's a beautiful Sunday morning in North Myrtle Beach and Emily Bowen, a wife and mother of four, lies dying on the beach. Jake Stellar returns in Beach Shoot, a new mystery by Rodney Riesel.

Beach Shoot is the second Jake Stellar book and sequel to the Amazon Best Seller North Murder Beach. In Beach Shoot, Jake finds himself teamed up with the most unlikely of partners, his nemesis and fellow detective Avis Lint. Join Jake and Avis as they piece together the clues in this thrilling new mystery.

ISBN: 978-0-9894877-5-7

Return to Dunquin Cove

The Dunquin Cove Series

Return to Dunquin Cove, the sequel to The Man in Room Number Four, is the second book in The Dunquin Cove series.

It's been almost six months since the day ex-hitman, Ben Dunning turned up in Dunquin Cove, Maine, not knowing where or who he was. He's lived a quiet, peaceful life in the small town, but now his old life is calling him back. As Ben plans a trip to Boston in search of his past, little does he know that trouble is brewing in Dunquin Cove. Two strangers have arrived with the promise of safety and security. Join Ben and the people of Dunquin Cove as they band together to prove they can take care of themselves and their town.

ISBN: 978-0-9894877-7-1